Making
Christmas

Ho Ho Uh-Oh!

This is the story of Kiernan McCrea (from *A Cowboy Wedding* and Cahill's brother from *A New World*) and Bexley Farber, who get caught at a shoddy convenience store in a Wyoming blizzard over Christmas. Their choice is to have one of the least festive Christmases on record or work with what they have and each other to make this a real Christmas for four stranded kids … and maybe discover what Santa has in mind for them.

5-Star Praise for *Making Christmas*
"Bexley, Kiernan and the amazing support cast in this book will steal your heart and light it up like a Christmas tree."

— Book Devil Reviews

MAKING CHRISTMAS

Wyoming Wildflowers series
Book 10

Patricia McLinn

Wyoming Wildflowers series

Wyoming Wildflowers: The Beginning (prequel)

Almost a Bride

Match Made in Wyoming

My Heart Remembers

A New World (prequel to Jack's Heart)

Jack's Heart

Rodeo Nights (prequel to Where Love Lives)

Where Love Lives

A Cowboy Wedding

Making Christmas

More romance by Patricia McLinn

Bardville, Wyoming series

A Stranger in the Family

A Stranger to Love

The Rancher Meets His Match

A Place Called Home series

Lost and Found Groom

At the Heart's Command

Hidden in a Heartbeat

Seasons in a Small Town series

The Wedding Series

Marry Me series

CHAPTER ONE

December 23

This was not a good idea, especially considering what happened five months and two days ago.

That was Bexley Farber's primary thought as they pulled away from the cluster of figures waving good-bye from the porch of the Slash -C(+15others) Ranch's main house.

As if Kiernan McCrea had heard her thought from the driver's seat, he abruptly said into the silence, "You sure you want to do this? I could take you back. You could spend the holidays safe and sound with the Curricks and all." He didn't look at her.

"So could you." She, too, looked straight out the windshield … except for the corner of her eye.

His mouth quirked. More a grimace than a smile. "Worth the risk to have Christmas with family, you know."

She stifled a reaction, remembering a reference to Kiernan and his family from the summer, which led to—Nope. Not going there, even in memory.

"I—" She cleared her froggy throat and started again. "I do know. That's why we're—I mean, each of us, individually, is making this trip."

"This mad trip."

She smiled tightly. "Not completely mad. Not as long as we stay ahead of the storm as you all plotted out."

"Aye. So we'd best be going. Unless you've changed your mind."

"No."

He accelerated onto the highway, heading north.

That revealed dark, heavy-bellied clouds to the west. The tops of the Big Horn Mountains seemed certain to tear open their bottoms, releasing a gush of snow.

Which matched the current forecast. Blizzard warnings starting tonight and continuing into Christmas Day.

It was the second of twin storms, moving from west to east across the country. The first twin reached the East Coast yesterday after knocking out Bexley's flight home. With so many scrambling for new flights she hadn't been able to get another one.

As Bexley knew now, this second system had threatened to trap Kiernan in San Francisco, where he'd been for business. He got out just in time, on a flight to Denver. But then stalled there, because no flights could get into his destination of Boston. Or anywhere near it.

In a flurry of phone calls, his family in Gloucester, on the coast north and east of Boston, told him not to risk it. To rent a vehicle in Denver and get up to Wyoming, where he could spend Christmas with the Curricks, close friends of the family.

He did rent this four-wheel drive and he did make the trip to the Slash-C last night. But according to his explanation this morning at breakfast, as he'd listened to the news and weather reports along the way yesterday, a different plan formed.

He'd drive the thirty-some hours to Boston, far enough behind the first storm to have cleared roads and far enough ahead of the second to not be caught.

The Curricks and their friends, who'd arrived for an impromptu welcome breakfast for Kiernan, were divided down the middle about whether it was a good idea or—as Donna Currick, the family's grande dame, said—a *mad plan.*

Then Matty Brennan Currick, married to Donna's son, Dave, and a hearty endorser of his plan, said, "And you'll take Bexley with, since her flights were all canceled, too, after she came here to do winter videos for her business. That will give you company and a second driver as far as Chicago."

"Chicago? But your family's in Wisco—" Kiernan cut it off mid-sentence.

Amid explanations about how Bexley had planned to connect to a train to her hometown south of Milwaukee after flying into Chicago, so she could do the same after driving, then Dave's suggestion they pick up I-94 in Madison, take it to her hometown, and Kiernan could stay on it to resume his eastern route, which prompted lots of map-checking, no one seemed to notice Kiernan's knowledge of her family's location.

Except Donna, Bexley thought.

Better Donna than her daughter-in-law, Matty, who had a tendency toward matchmaking. All with the best intentions, but the last thing Bexley wanted was being matched with Kiernan McCrea.

The second-to-the-last thing was being shut up in a vehicle with him for seventeen-plus hours.

She wasn't quite sure how she'd ended up here … except for the longing to be with her family for Christmas. An instinct to get home, to get to family that gripped so much of the population that from the right angle, the earth would probably look like a teeming ant hill, with streams going one direction and other streams just as determinedly going different directions.

With the urgency of the instinct, the encouragement of the driving plan backers, and the looming deadline of the incoming storm, she'd quickly repacked the belonging she'd need for the trip, and let herself be bundled into the big, comfortable four-wheel drive.

Like a spelunker following a rope back out of a cave to daylight, she tried to retrace how all that happened. But she kept losing the thread in conversational side caverns. Consultations of weather forecasts, storm warnings, road conditions. Memories of past blizzards. Cautions about handling Wyoming winter roads. Donations of equipment and supplies for winter driving.

No spelunker would ever make it out of a cave that busy and cha-otic.

Kiernan slowed the vehicle for a turn to the east.

With the dark clouds hidden from view behind them and a brighter prospect before them, Bexley's spirits lifted slightly.

However it happened, she was on her way now—headed *home*.

In a car for seventeen-plus hours with Kiernan McCrea.

Bexley raised her gloved hands as if to adjust the hood on her jacket, allowing her to take a sideways look at the profile of the man in the driver's seat without being too obvious.

This was not a good idea.

Seventeen and a half hours in a vehicle with Kiernan McCrea. That's if they didn't take breaks, didn't stop for meals, didn't stop for … rest.

She closed her eyes.

Maybe she could sleep from Wyoming to Wisconsin. Except for when she took her turns driving, of course. She could volunteer to do lots of the driving, since he'd face a dozen or more hours to go after dropping her off.

No need for conversation or strained silence if he slept.

The presence of Kiernan McCrea, sleeping beside her.

Her breath hitched.

This was *really* not a good idea.

Especially considering what happened five months and two days ago.

CHAPTER TWO

Five months and two days ago

Something about Kiernan McCrea snagged Bexley's attention the first time she saw him, standing on the back porch of the Currick ranch house, looking out to the Big Horn Mountains as if he could read them.

And it wasn't the tall, dark, and handsome thing he had going with thick, wavy hair that always appeared as if tossed by a breeze from his native Ireland.

Because she wasn't looking at him—wasn't looking at *any* man—that way. She'd sworn off men. Probably for good. Certainly for the rest of this year and into the next, because eighteen months of no men struck her as a nice round number and a good start on what she needed to do.

To heal. To get back to herself. To forget the past and forge a future. On. Her. Own.

So, what about this guy caught her attention?

Despite very limited exposure to him.

First, because he rarely stopped working from what she could tell. Second, because when he was dragged—and he clearly had to be dragged—into social gatherings that gave them occasion to speak to each other, he never even made eye contact.

And then she had it.

Kiernan McCrea was an outlier on the Slash-C Ranch.

The slight Irish accent set him apart, of course, but more than that, he wasn't friendly. In fact, he was downright dour, entirely unlike the people who lived on the Slash-C and visited here.

That made Kiernan McCrea stand out.

And it was weird, because in the beat when their eyes met for the first time, she'd thought… She'd been wrong. Way wrong.

He hadn't even smiled when they were introduced. Just a curt nod. Then, the first few times she'd crossed paths with him on the ranch and said a cheery hello, he'd looked right through her.

Made her shiver. And not in a good way. Not that she was up for any shivering in a good way, because she wasn't. Sworn off men. Until into the new year.

Didn't mean she couldn't be curious—on a strictly academic basis.

Kiernan McCrea was a definite outlier on the Slash-C.

Though not an outsider, as she was.

When she'd arrived in Wyoming, she'd known only Val.

Val—Valerie Trimarco Ralston—had invited Bexley to come to the Slash-C Ranch, where her husband, Jack, was foreman. Perhaps an unlikely spot to work on launching an online business, but no way was Bexley turning down the invitation.

Val ran a successful business that started as a mommy blog and grew into online courses and communities. Bexley met her through intersecting interests in building online communities, though Bexley's had been for young DINKs—Dual Income, No Kids—while Val helped overwhelmed mothers, especially single mothers. They met virtually, later in person, forming a friendship, then a closer friendship, and now a business association.

Val was kicking her backside to create a new online presence after her previous one imploded. Along with her relationship, her self-esteem, and her sense of who she was. … Or had that last one slo-mo imploded long before her ex declared his ex-ness in one stunning and abrupt hour almost a year ago.

It had taken arriving at the Slash-C for Bexley to realize one of the things she still held against Nigel was his timing.

If he'd dumped his bombshell a couple months earlier, she'd have been here for Val and Jack's wedding last summer and she wouldn't have been such an outsider now.

Instead, Nigel refused to consider going to a wedding in Wyoming. He hadn't precisely said he didn't want her to go. But she'd been in the misguided mindset that it was the two of them sailing through the world together. She'd given up the idea of attending.

All part of the package of being together … or so she'd thought at the time.

So, here she was now, an outsider with an itch of curiosity about the outlier.

But if she asked about him, Val would pounce. And Val would *not* let go.

Bexley had known that, but, boy, knowing and feeling it first-hand while they worked together were two different things.

Far safer to let the itch go unscratched.

But then, a couple weeks into her stay and four days after Kiernan's arrival, Bexley was helping Matty Brennan Currick with the final cleanup in the kitchen after a casual cookout dinner.

Val, Jack, their daughter, Addie, and their eight-month-old son, Mick, had gone home earlier to the foreman's house a few miles away because Jack had been up all night with a newly arrived rescue horse. Dave and Kiernan were cleaning the grill outside—when Dave wasn't catching his screaming-with-delight kids with the hose's stream.

Bexley, putting away a serving dish on the shelves in the eating area, looked out the patio doors, chuckling at the scene.

Kiernan, grinning at what was going on around him, looked up toward her and for half a second she could almost think—Then his expression settled into familiar lines proclaiming she was some kind of enemy. Before he dropped his head and resumed scrubbing.

Matty, looking out the window over the sink at the horseplay, clicked her tongue. But she was smiling with her whole face. "At least Kiernan's working out there."

Her smile faded.

"I should say at least Kiernan took a break from working to come to dinner tonight. He's *always* working these days."

With perfect neutrality, Bexley said, "Isn't he here for a working visit, like me?"

"You don't need to work so hard, either," Matty scolded. "But at least Val gets you to join in with a few of the fun things."

"Like the ride and picnic last weekend. That was amazing."

Matty grinned, taking a pitcher Bexley had dried and putting it away in a far cupboard. "It was fun. I wish Kiernan had been here then. As it is, he hasn't let up since he arrived."

"The computer system, isn't it?" Bexley had picked that up from casual conversation with a couple of the cowhands.

They'd also said Kiernan spent a lot of time out on the range, testing devices under ranching conditions.

"Yes. He stopped here on his way from the West Coast to Boston for his real job because he said he had software for us to test—except then he's insisted on doing all the testing. Working, working, working."

Matty broke off.

"Not that I'm complaining. We're so fortunate he's taken over our computer system. He revamped it a while back and it's made a huge difference. Now he swings by periodically and checks, updates, and tweaks it, so it's better every time. Or he does one of these bigger overhauls, like now."

"How did he start working for the Slash-C?"

"Oh, Kiernan is family." Matty looked out the window again, this time not focusing on her husband and kids. "You know, he's so far up there in the software world we couldn't possibly afford his services if he'd let us pay him, which he won't. I just wish he'd have some fun."

In one way, Bexley could see Kiernan McCrea being part of the Currick family, she thought later as she neared the mini house where Currick family members stayed when they visited, but generously turned over for her use now.

He acted like family with the adults, but especially with the kids.

Though Bexley did wonder how the Irish branch worked into the Currick family tree. Or was it Matty's? She was born a Brennan, so maybe that was the connection.

Maybe she'd do a little sleuthing on her laptop tonight. She'd gotten into the habit of taking the laptop to bed with her—appreciating a faithful bed companion. Nothing intrusive, a little dip into publicly posted information—

Darn.

She'd left her laptop in the ranch office where she and Val were working when they were called for dinner.

She turned around and headed back to the office.

Good. The inside door stood open as she and Val left it—intending to do more after dinner, until good company, good conversation, and Jack's need for sleep changed their plans. The screen door would still be open. Yep. A few steps to the desk, pick up her laptop and—

Kiernan McCrea stood at the desk, looking down at the notes and sketches she and Val had made during their work session.

At some point, she'd heard he slept in the ranch office. But seeing no sign of his occupation the times she and Val worked here with baby Mick napping nearby, she'd forgotten that piece of information until this moment.

He was barefoot and his shirt was unbuttoned, revealing a slice of chest and flat abdomen.

The sight heated her breath and froze her brain.

"Oh."

She felt wrong-footed. Partly by surprise. Partly by the guilty knowledge of thinking about digging into his family connection to the Curricks. Partly by—

No. Not until the new year.

Prepared to abandon her laptop for now, she started to turn away as she'd done regularly since he'd rebuffed her overtures.

But with him being related to Matty and her likely to cross paths with him again if she was invited back to the Slash-C—which she hoped she would be, because not only was it a wonderful place with terrific people, current company excepted, but she'd such made great strides in creating a new online business under Val's talented kicking—she'd make more of an effort.

"Hi, Kiernan. Forgot my laptop before dinner. Sorry if I intruded. Didn't know you were here or I'd have knocked."

He barely flicked her a look, grunted, and continued looking at the notes and sketches. He even extended one hand down to graze the papers with his fingertips, nudging one to better see what was beneath it.

Her notes and sketches.

Well, hers and Val's. But for *her* new online business. In some ways for her new self.

The edifice she'd built around the *lifestyle* she lived with Nigel had proven all polish and fluff. Why, oh why, in the few times Nigel consented to spend time with her family, hadn't she paid attention to their reaction? Her parents' polite distance, her siblings' guarded distrust, including her younger brother's crack she wasn't supposed to hear about Nigel resembling a glossy magazine you'd flip through in a waiting room, but wouldn't bring home.

She'd thought at the time their reaction was because he had so much more polish and experience of the world than her family, which he'd pointed out with stiff amusement.

She'd eventually learned it was because, dazzled by the polish, she'd missed the minimal substance beneath.

Not ever again.

Not in her personal life. Not in her business life.

This plan had substance. Because it was based on *her*—core elements of her that had survived Nigel's gloss offensive and would survive. No matter what.

Val helped her find a way to help people with what she knew. Not create a *lifestyle*, but build a better life. A real life.

"I see you're looking at what Val's helping me put together for my new online business. Planning all the pieces—videos, classes, website, podcast. Starting to put them together."

Another grunt.

Forget friendly. Kiernan McCrea wasn't even polite.

A *grunt*. For all their hard work. For all she hoped for—

Not that he owed her anything. But what about Val's work and creativity? And how about his *family*? Showing him so much love while he sat there through dinner like a lump of coal.

Hands on hips, she demanded, "So, how *are* you related to Matty?"

If he picked up a strong inference that the only conceivable reason his miserable self would be allowed to be around the fine people of the

Slash-C was nepotism added to their inexplicable generosity in his case, she could live with that.

"Matty?" His dark brows drove down without narrowing his eyes to the point of obscuring their distinctive green.

"She said you're family," she said, none too patiently, because his lack of understanding wasn't from lack of brains, making it more likely it was from lack of interest in anything she said.

He looked up, staring. Not seeing her—clearly—for several beats. He blinked and it was like light came on inside him. It dazzled her. The way a match flame could in a dark room.

And then he laughed.

She could swear it vibrated through her nerves and reverberated in her bones.

"Related? Try her ranch foreman's wife's cousin's brother-in-law—no, wait. It's worse, because Jack officially started as the Curricks' foreman, so I'm her husband's ranch foreman's wife's cousin's husband's brother. *That's* Matty's definition of family."

She could not help chuckling back—strictly for Matty, not for him, since he had a lot of sourpuss to make up for.

Maybe also for herself, because chuckling was a heck of a lot less disconcerting than vibrating.

"Matty's husband's ranch's foreman." By repeating the words, she started to follow along the thread he'd drawn. "So, that's Jack. And his wife's Val."

"Right. Val's cousin, Eleanor, married my brother Cahill. They're not here, but they come to visit regularly with their kids."

She stepped through it again with care, trying to get it straight in her head. "Matty's husband's foreman's wife's—" Matty, Dave, Jack, and Val, all people she knew. Now she ventured into unknown territory, though she'd certainly heard about them from Val. "—cousin's husband's—"

"That's Eleanor, who's Val's cousin, and Cahill, who's my—"

"Brother," they ended together.

He laughed.

She laughed.

Way past what it deserved, maybe. Making up for his coldness to her, her prickliness toward him, probably.

Laughed long enough and hard enough to feel like ribcages had shrunk.

Looking at each other as they tried to replenish oxygen levels.

That was one instant.

In the next, that match flame in the dark ignited something entirely unexpected. Something volatile.

Oxygen still depleted, but now because the fire of his look consumed every bit around her.

Impossible.

Yet she felt her breasts rising and falling faster and faster with the need to pull in air.

No, no, no, no, no. This was not possible.

He raised his hands, half reaching for her.

She didn't move.

He dropped his hands. Stepped back.

They stayed put. More distance between them. Safer distance between them.

Except his breathing was as bad as hers. And eye contact? She might combust from the eye contact alone.

One of them had to look away. Now.

His green-eyed gaze holding hers, he surged forward, his hands bracketing her upturned face, his fingers driving into her hair. Then his mouth on hers. His tongue inside. And hers exploring him. Tasting. Delving.

His one hand cupped the back of her head. The other came to her shoulder.

"Bexley."

Talking meant a sliver of space between them. No longer heartbeat to heartbeat. Enough for sense to return.

Her hand was high on his chest, spanning his open shirt. Her fingers bunched the fabric. She tugged him toward her.

CHAPTER THREE

December 23

"Bexley, wake up. We've a problem."

She couldn't have been deeply asleep, because she responded the instant Kiernan said her name. And she already knew the vehicle had stopped. Yet straightening up and looking around, shock jolted her. Someone had dumped a gazillion flour bags over the world and was still dumping.

She leaned forward, hoping it would help her see through the white in the instant wipers contacted a slice of the windshield. For an instant, she thought Kiernan had nudged her, then she realized the whole vehicle rocked from the wind.

"Road's closed." Kiernan nodded to the bar across the road and a sign, each appearing for a flicker as the wipers passed.

Road? The *world* looked like it had closed.

"But—"

A knock on the driver's window interrupted.

Kiernan lowered the window, where snow rapidly collected.

"Road ahead's closed. Can't go any farther." An official voice came from an oddly shaped snowman under a frosted trooper's hat.

"But the forecast—" Bexley started, trying to assimilate this new reality.

"Weather didn't get the forecast memo," the official voice rumbled.

"Can we go back and go around the worst of this, north or south?" Kiernan asked.

The hat twirled a fall of snow with a head shake.

"We'll have to go back to the Curricks'."

She said it mostly to herself. Better or worse than remaining in the car alone with Kiernan? Both. Better with more people around them. Worse with too many of those people trying to push them together.

Another twirl of snow indicated another head shake. "No going back. Westbound's closed, too. You'll follow me to shelter and stay there until we say otherwise."

"How far is it?" Kiernan asked.

"Down the road from the exit. Keep my rear lights in sight, but don't ride my bumper."

The snowman trudged away.

"Nothing for it but to do as he says," Kiernan said.

"When did this start?"

"It was snowing for a while. After the previous exit it started coming down like a pillow ripped open. When I could see the country around, it looked like it had been going for some time. I hoped it was a bad pocket we'd get through. But it kept getting worse."

She started to ask more, but saw Kiernan's deep concentration on driving as the trooper's vehicle pulled in front of them, with emergency lights flashing.

Down the exit, they started. At the bottom, the rear end of the vehicle wanted to take a different path, but Kiernan persuaded it back in time to make the turn onto the highway behind the trooper. The interstate passed above them, buffering some of the wind and snow for a few moments. Which seemed to make both all the stronger when they left the relative protection of the underpass.

"Where's he headed? There's nothing," Kiernan muttered. "Nothing a'tall."

Bexley leaned forward. "I think I see ... something. A roof, maybe?"

Through the snow, a shape like an upside down V appeared on the left side of the road.

"Can't even try to look," he said.

"No, don't. But I do think there's something ahead on the left side of the road. Yes! The trooper turned his indicator on."

The trooper pulled into a snow-covered lot, bypassing where a single gas pump stood lonely, snow-shrouded sentry, and stopping in front of a building, leaving a space between his vehicle and a four-wheel drive with Wyoming plates.

Kiernan steered after him. Bexley felt the wind try to shove them sideways, but Kiernan kept in the trooper's tire tracks. Until they pushed across fresh snow to park in the space.

She looked at Kiernan. He looked at her. Quickly, they both looked back at the building visible through the windshield.

The driving snow didn't help the view much. Through it, they saw what appeared to be two small buildings smashed together. Both had rock facades, with short, rectangular windows under the low eaves of sharply peaked roofs. Each had a door in the center with a peaked eave over it, though the door on the right appeared to be boarded up. The building on the left had a dark gray roof, the one on the right rusty red in the few places snow didn't cover. That right-hand roof sat significantly lower than the other, making it appear the runt of this two-building litter.

To either side of the operable door were snow-covered lumps. A flap of blue indicated a tarp had covered something there before it was mostly covered in turn by snow.

The trooper left his vehicle running. As they exited Kiernan's rental, the trooper shouted, "Get your things."

A sound came to her. Familiar, but she couldn't immediately identify it as the wind whipped it away.

"We're staying here? At a gas station?" Bexley asked as she and Kiernan met at the back of the vehicle. She squinted into the snow, trying to locate the source of the sound. She could make out the outlines of a pickup with a trailer behind it.

Kiernan pulled out her bag and held onto it as he got his own as well. "Not much of a gas station, either. Would you bring that shopping bag in? Things in there might freeze."

"I can carry my suitcase…" Remembering its weight and accepting there'd be no rolling the suitcase in the accumulating snow, she let her protest die and accepted the help. "I'll get the shopping bag and close up."

"Don't. I'll come back for the gear the Curricks stowed. If we're to stay here any time a'tall, we'll need it."

The trooper opened the building's door from inside as they arrived. Kiernan left what he'd carried and went back immediately.

"What's he doing?"

"More gear," was all Bexley could get out as she maneuvered herself and her load out of the way of the door.

Kiernan returned before she had her breath back.

The trooper opened the door again, then pulled it closed immediately, winning a tussle with the wind.

With Kiernan safely inside, Bexley looked around.

CHAPTER FOUR

They'd stepped into a crowded shop with rows of shoulder-high shelves hugging narrow aisles. The back showed ranks of glass doors to cold storage, the right side held more racks until reaching an opening at the back that must connect to the shorter building next door. The left side held the counter to check out, with a microwave and a trio of coffee machines in the corner beyond it.

An older woman in a bright blue sweater was filling a thermos at one of the coffee machines.

The sudden cessation of snow and wind hit Bexley first. She supposed warmth would seep in more slowly to defrost bones frozen in the short trip to the door.

An attractive fair-haired man in his mid-thirties, wearing quality casual clothes, stepped forward and helpfully took one of the bags from Kiernan and the shopping bag from her.

"More people? More darned people?" came a harsh voice from behind the counter near the door. "Already bursting."

"It's these folks and the earlier two, other than your family." The trooper's hat tipped toward a group gathered by the opening at the right rear, presumably leading to the other half of the building.

Another man in his mid-thirties, also attractive yet of an entirely different type, stood there with four kids. He wore old, working jeans, with an open jacket showing layers of clothes beneath it. He held a cowboy hat with damp marks spotted on it and a puddle beneath it, signaling it had carried a crop of snow.

The kids ranged around him. A lanky boy barely in his teens. Two girls half the boy's age who looked enough alike to be twins. One of them held a toddler of two, maybe three years old.

"*His* family. He'll tell you so soon enough," the voice from behind the counter said in apparent reference to the man holding his hat.

Bexley leaned forward to look past Kiernan and saw the voice came from an older man with clashing plaid flannel shirts, one atop the other, patches of solid white and salt-and-pepper hair sticking out at even odder angles than her first ever attempt with styling gel produced, and a slightly lighter-colored beard bushing out from his cheeks, then scraggled toward two uneven points down his chest.

Tension seemed to zing from the man behind the counter to the family group and back.

"What the he—heck's with this snow anyway? Weren't supposed to get this storm for another twelve hours," the older man grumbled.

"Still coming," the trooper said. "This is a bonus, not the main storm. Some front moved in when it wasn't supposed to and met up with another front and—" He held his hands together, palms up, then jerked them apart, allowing whatever mythical something they'd held to drop. "—*bloop*."

"These are the last of the eastbounders," he continued. "All other vehicles accounted for. I'm going back west to check if anyone's stranded."

"And because your family's there," the shopkeeper said cynically.

"That, too. Gives me a chance to be home for Christmas," he said cheerfully.

Home for Christmas.

The hope got Bexley into the vehicle with Kiernan, made him plan to drive three-quarters of the way across the country, brought them here.

Oh-so-far from home for Christmas.

The trooper had a question for the shopkeeper. "How're you situated on propane? Got enough?"

"I got plenty for *me*. Could run right through it with the battalion you've dumped on me."

The older woman came toward them, tightening the top on a thermos with quick, competent movements.

"You'll have to make do. Maybe ration it out. You all—" The

trooper's gaze went from the woman offering the thermos, to the blond man with her, then to Kiernan, over to the family group by the door, finally to Bexley. "—stay here until we get you word it's safe to go."

"Stay here. Stay here. Like I'm running a ritzy hotel at Grand Central Station," the bearded shopkeeper grumbled.

"Yeah. Exactly like that," the trooper said dryly. Then he looked at the man with the cowboy hat. Bexley, following his gaze, saw shadows under the man's eyes, grooves dug in around his mouth. Weariness, worry, and worn down. "Everybody stays here. It's too dangerous out there to try to get anywhere. Won't be anybody can get to you to help if you go in a ditch."

The man said nothing. Nor did he meet the trooper's gaze. The trooper muttered something, put his hat and gloves back on, took the refilled thermos from the woman with a nod, and left without another word.

For a long moment, no one moved.

Then the woman who'd filled the thermos, extended a hand to Bexley. "I'm Pauline Ohlrich and this is Eric Larkin. We're stranded, too. Couldn't get far enough east fast enough to miss the storm. And our charming host said everyone calls him Gramps. I suspect he misheard them calling him Grump."

She not only said it loud enough for the man behind the counter to hear, she made a point of looking at him as she said it.

A faint ripple showed in his unruly beard which might have been from a grimace. On the other hand it might not have been aimed at the woman named Pauline.

As Bexley and Kiernan completed introductions with Pauline and Eric, the shopkeeper stomped over to the family group.

The two men's voices didn't rise, but the intensity came through.

"—you're the last person on earth I'd want to see here, Hall Quick. And with all them in tow."

"Last place on earth I'd want to be or to bring them to. No choice." The father of the family group jerked his head in the direction of the window. "Can't risk taking them further in this."

"You're worried more about those animals than—"

"If I don't get them to where I can sell them—" He stopped, clearly not willing to consider it. "I'm going. No choice. I'll be back for the kids as soon as I can."

"I don't want—"

"Don't worry. They won't look to you for anything more than you'd give a stranger." He turned to his family. "Dan—"

The teenage boy didn't look up. "I know."

"—you're responsible for the others."

"But, Daddy," said one of the girls, "we have to be home for Christmas. You'll be back to get us and take us home for Christmas."

The lines by his mouth deepened. He jerked his head in a sharp negative. "Don't see how that can happen, Molly."

Tears came to the other girl's eyes. "But you'll be back *here* by Christmas, even if we're not home, you'll be here with us for Christmas, won't you?"

"Probably not." His voice went even grimmer and rougher. "We'll have to let Christmas go by this year, Lizzie. I'll be back as soon as I can."

He cupped his hand over the head of the three younger children, one by one, started his hand toward the oldest, then drew it back when the boy called Dan recoiled. He gave his son a nod.

The man clapped the hat on his head, then fastened his jacket as he walked to the door. Did his boots make his footsteps sound like they belonged to a much heavier man? Pulling the door open, he hesitated an instant, then, without looking back, he disappeared into the opaque world beyond.

No one had moved when they heard, under the wind, the low sound of a truck engine laboring to life.

The truck with a trailer.

The familiar sound she'd heard had come from cattle in the trailer, Bexley realized.

She hadn't spent a lot of time in Wyoming, but knew that wasn't the regulation size cattle transport trailer. It wouldn't carry many head. For the man to risk going out in this because he absolutely had to get those few head to market must mean a precarious financial situation.

The storekeeper turned his head to look out the window. "Well, by the lights, he's made it onto the highway. Doubt the fool will make it much farther."

The boy named Dan glared a hole in the back of the older man's head.

Oblivious, the shopkeeper said, "No use waiting around to see. How about some coffee?"

The last was not an offer to the rest of them, but was directed at the older woman with a jerk of his head toward a cup on the counter as an apparent request for a refill.

"Get your own. We need to settle these newcomers in. And considering what you *didn't* do for us or your relatives by way of welcoming and settling in, I'll see to that."

"The first thing for me is to point me toward the restroom, please," Bexley said.

"A door in here says Women." The girl holding the little boy tipped her head toward the room behind her.

"Next to one saying Men," her sister added.

CHAPTER FIVE

Bexley passed the four children at the doorway to the other room, smiling at them all. The little boy smiled back. The girls stared, not unfriendly. The teenager ignored her.

The room she stepped into was chilly, dim, and dusty except for a pile of belongings—had to be the kids', considering it included the biggest box of pull-up diapers she'd ever seen—leaning against the wall by the doorway, which was flanked by grubby curtain panels.

She squinted, not sure she could make out the far wall.

"Over there." The girl holding the little boy shifted him in order to free one hand and point.

The little boy contributed his chubby arm to signpost duty, too. "Dare."

Turning her squint in that direction, Bexley saw faint lettering on two doors to her left, then a third door in the corner with no lettering.

"Thank you."

Crossing the room quickly, she pushed open the door marked "Women."

She returned on the outward swing and made it back across the room twice as fast.

"I thought you had to—"

She swept past Kiernan, now standing in the back aisle of the store near the coffee maker, with a crisp, "I do."

She also swept past the shopkeeper named Gramps and into the shelves of the store area.

Pauline groaned. "Should have known. Eric, we might need your help."

"Should have known what?" Gramps asked. "What do you think

you're doing?"

Not answering or slowing in her gathering of cleaning supplies, Bexley asked, "Where's your mop?"

"Here's a new one," Pauline said, passing it to Eric. "And hold this."

She took the supplies Bexley had gathered and started to hand those to Eric, too, but Kiernan stepped in and took them. Bexley was already reloading.

"We'll need the new mop, but for the first pass, an old one will do." Bexley leveled a look at the shopkeeper over the top of the shelves.

He mumbled two or three sentences of complaint, but finished with, "In the closet by the restrooms."

With Bexley in front, then Pauline, Kiernan, Eric, and followed at a grumbling distance by the shopkeeper, they trooped past the kids in the doorway and back into the room next to the shop. Bexley headed for the door with no lettering, the best bet for a closet.

She opened it wide, reaching around to capture what appeared to be a pull string for a light.

And jerked her arm back.

The *string* was actually cobweb. The closet looked like a Halloween decoration of fake spiderwebs, except the webs festooning a mop, broom, bucket, and other artifacts of ancient cleaning rituals were all too real.

In the meantime, Pauline had pushed open the door to the women's room. Like Bexley, she didn't linger.

On her immediate return, she confronted Gramps.

"How on earth can you offer these facilities to people?"

"Don't offer them. Don't *want* people stopping here to use the facilities. Most folks who come here live close enough to use their own da—darned facilities. Besides, it was people using the facilities that got them in this state to start with."

"A decade ago," Pauline said grimly. "And since we're all going to be here for a few days, there are going to need to be changes around here."

Here for a few days.

Without consulting her about it, Bexley's head turned toward Kiernan.

From the instant she'd awakened to the news the road was closed, she'd focused on their next immediate step to get out of the storm.

Now the reality that they were likely to be here for several days hit.

With home a long day's drive away in good weather, the line from the song *I'll Be Home for Christmas* that applied to her was *if only in my dreams.*

"We'll have to let people know we're stuck here." Her eyes stung. Mom and Dad would be so disappointed. The rest of the family, too. Almost as disappointed as she was.

A vision of her family home, festively decorated and smelling of evergreens and cookies, flashed bright and warm.

Kiernan's family, too. They'd all be gathered in Gloucester, Massachusetts. Without him. He had to be as disappointed as she was.

Suddenly seventeen hours in a car with him didn't seem such a bad prospect. Especially if it had gotten them each home.

He nodded grimly, confirming Pauline's forecast, acknowledging Bexley's dismay.

Before it was clear if Kiernan would have said anything, Gramps erupted.

"*Changes around here?* What changes? Bad enough I have to have all you people here for days when I don't want you, but—"

"Days? But it's two days to Christmas. If we're here for *days...* We're all going to be here for *Christmas?*" The question rose toward a wail. Bexley felt as if the girl her father called Lizzie channeled her inner reaction.

"Of course we are," Dan snapped, rolling his eyes. "What did you not understand about Dad saying, no, he wouldn't be back for Christmas? And we're letting Christmas go by this year?"

"But... But..."

Molly, the girl holding the little boy, blurted out the fear behind her sister's repeated syllables. "How will Santa Claus find us *here?*"

"Santa Claus always knows where to find good children," Bexley said.

Where had *that* come from? Was she channeling her mother? Bexley touched each girl on her shoulder, then saw she'd trailed cobwebs along, and quickly tucked it into her fist before the girls noticed.

"Not here," Gramps said. "No Santa Claus ever came here."

"He will this year," Bexley said firmly.

Pauline sent the shopkeeper a teeth-bared grimace, then turned a pleasant but no-nonsense expression on the girls. "But first we have to make sure he finds a clean establishment."

"Absolutely." Ignoring the spiderwebs, Bexley quickly pulled out the old broom.

As she reached for the mop handle, steeling herself for the cobwebby feel, Kiernan shouldered in next to her. "I'll get it."

He grasped the handle and used it to also drag the bucket out. With a gesture, he indicated he'd take it into the restroom for them. Bexley went first, holding the women's room door open for him, followed by Pauline.

He muttered something. Sounded like a curse, though not a word she recognized. "Do you want me to—?"

"Clean the whole thing yourself?" she interrupted, shaking cobwebs off the gray and stringy mop head. "Oh, yes, I do. I really, *really* do. But I can't imagine the men's is any better. Save yourself for that."

"Eric will help you, Kiernan." Pauline turned on a faucet in the sink where the graphite gray of dirt was relieved by rust stains. The faucet spat and hawked like a cat trying to get up a hairball, then produced a small but steady stream of passable water. "Before you go, check the commode."

"The—?"

"Toilet," Bexley translated, applying the dry mop first to the ceiling, and a small window set high in the wall. She did not want to be surprised by those things falling on her head.

Behind her, she heard Kiernan jangle the toilet handle, then a recognizable flush.

Pauline commented, "Hope you're as lucky on your side. Now, get out of here. We'll have to work fast to keep from freezing and it's too tight to work fast with three of us when one's the size of you, Kiernan."

"I'll go, but before I do… Bexley, you can't promise those kids what you can't deliver. That talk of Santa…"

Bexley didn't turn around, focusing intently on the cobwebs above her.

After a moment, she heard the door open and close behind him.

"He has a point, you know," Pauline said.

She did know.

So she'd just have to deliver. Somehow.

CHAPTER SIX

Bexley and Pauline finished the women's room—uncovering a white sink no one would call bright white—and gladly started on the main room, because it wasn't quite as cold as the women's room. The shopkeeper clearly didn't waste any money heating this side of the building. And not much on the shop side, either.

While they'd worked, Pauline had told her Eric was a lawyer in Bardville, Wyoming, and her employer.

Their relationship seemed closer. Pauline certainly showed no sign of deferring to a boss.

Perhaps noticing Bexley's surprise, Pauline expanded.

"Guess you could say we bonded from the start. He was opening his practice and he took a risk on a new widow with no work history, who'd been turned down for jobs dozens of times. He's a good man. And he got a real raw deal in the relationship department. When he decided to listen to a few friends he had out here and start all over in Wyoming, I wasn't about to let him do it on his own, whatever he said."

Her decisive conclusion matched Bexley's brief observations so well she bit back a grin.

As Bexley and Pauline switched to the new cleaning supplies from the old mop and bucket, they passed those tools to Kiernan and Eric to start on the men's room.

Now, they had the first-pass tools back for the main room.

Pauline apparently took it as an accepted fact they would clean the outer room.

Bexley hadn't thought about it.

Not until she saw those four kids, seated on the floor, using their bags as backrests, except for the small boy, who sat in the lap of one of the girls.

Fine.

They were cleaning the main room, too.

The first task, though, was putting working light bulbs—supplied from the shelves of the shop over Gramps' protests—in an overhead wagon wheel fixture hanging off-center over the empty area of the room. Bexley started by standing on a stool.

More light allowed them to see a wood stove occupied the corner opposite the door. The wall next to the stove had an odd texture… Bexley stared hard to make out dingy hubcaps hanging in incomplete rows across it.

A dark bar ran along much of the front side of the room with more stools upside down on top of it and two narrow windows high on the wall behind it, with shelves holding murky bottles between them. Four tables hugged the back wall, similarly decorated by upside down chairs of varied design.

Pauline put Dan to work searching out more places needing light-bulbs, with his sister, Lizzie, as his bulb-holding assistant. Pauline began sorting items from behind the bar into a garbage bin.

Gramps took a chair down from a table and planted himself in it, silently refusing to help.

Molly settled the shopkeeper's hash by plunking her little brother into his lap and refusing to heed his calls for her to come back and take the kid, who appeared fascinated with his beard. Instead, Molly took up the nearly dry mop and started on the cobwebs she could reach.

"All done, Pauline," Eric reported, emerging from the men's room, followed by Kiernan. "Hey, be careful up there, Becky."

He hurried to where she stood on the bar stool, now batting down cobwebs from around the light fixture with a broom. They weren't nearly as thick here, but still had a tendency to droop down to the level of unsuspecting heads.

"Thanks, I'm fine. Tested all the stools and took the steadiest. But it's Bexley—B-e-x-l-e-y. Not Becky."

"Sorry. Bexley. Want me to take over up there?"

She smiled down at him. "Everybody does it. No worries."

He smiled back.

He had a nice smile. Warm without being over the top. A little sad.

Her gaze slid toward Kiernan. His smile wasn't so much sad as closed off. Except for…

She refocused on Eric, picking up their exchange. "You have good timing. I just finished."

"So there's nothing left for us to do." Eric winked at her. A wait-for-it wink, predicting what was about to happen.

"There's plenty still to be done," Pauline immediately contradicted.

Eric grinned at his prediction coming true.

These two clearly knew each other well—to predict the older woman's behavior, but to tease about it.

Bexley returned his grin. "You and Kiernan can use the mop and this broom to get the cobwebs high up on the walls and ceiling where Molly and I didn't reach. She and I will start washing up the area of the bar Pauline's cleared."

Pauline had discovered a working faucet and small sink behind the bar, which would make that easier.

"What is this place?" Molly asked.

"Used to be a bar." Dan screwed in a bulb in one of two sconces flanking the doorway to the shop.

"Still is a bar," Gramps snapped. "A closed bar. Where nobody's supposed to be."

Pauline didn't let that pass. "If you cleaned it, you wouldn't need to be ashamed of it. Bring me the glass from those sconces, Dan, so I can wash them and the light can show through."

"I'm not ashamed of it."

She retorted, "Well, you should be."

Bexley sputtered, covering her laughter with a cough. Accidental-ly—she was sure it was accidentally—her gaze met Kiernan's and saw the same amusement in his green eyes.

"Why'd you close the bar?" Molly asked.

"Tired of people asking me nosy questions."

Pursuing that response logically, she asked, "They can ask nosy questions in the store, too, so why do you still have that open?"

"Eating's a habit I can't break."

"You mean you need money," the girl said wisely. "But you could make more money with the bar open. And then you could eat better." She regarded him for an extra beat. "Clothes, too."

Before Gramps could respond to his tormentor, he had to snap his head around for a gentle-voiced attack from a new direction.

"Mommy said everybody used to like to come to your bar because there was lots of laughing. And people would play instruments and some would sing and others would dance. It used to be exciting." Lizzie looked over at him.

"Big excitement." Dan's disdainful sarcasm swamped his sister's sweetness.

"We get excitement. Had a vehicle practically running over the pump and crashing into the store last summer."

Dan rolled his eyes—again. "More like a lady fainting and coasting over the curb. *Excitement*. Too bad it didn't knock down the place."

Lizzie ignored her brother. "But why did you close someplace so wonderful? Mommy said it was really wonderful."

Bexley's mind buzzed with questions.

Where was their mother?

Mommy said. So their mother, as well as their father, knew this man. *Gramps.* Did that mean…?

"None of your business," the man snapped.

But not at her unvoiced question.

Lizzie jerked back as if struck.

Dan stepped in front of her. "Mom said you were a bitter, sour old man. The kind who'd pick on a little kid. That's why she'd never bring us here to see you."

"Well, you're here now, whether I want you or not and I sure as hell don't—"

"Yes, we are here, thanks to this blizzard," Pauline said briskly. "No use crying over spilled milk. We shall make the best of the situation. All of us."

Gramps showed no sign of recognizing the severe look she directed at him, but neither did he say more.

That would have to do.

CHAPTER SEVEN

Trying to ease the tension, Bexley asked the first thing into her mind, "Do you have more?"

"More what?"

"More grandchildren."

"Nah." Did that constitute confirmation they *were* his grandchildren?

"Our aunt doesn't have kids." Molly sighed, then kindly explained to Bexley, "We don't have any cousins."

She nodded solemnly, sucking in her cheeks to mask amusement.

"So, one of you gave him the name Gramps?"

Under her breath, Pauline suggested again, "Unless they meant Grump."

"That was Dan. Mommy told us. Remember, Lizzie?" Backed by her sister's nod, Molly continued, "Mommy used to bring Dan here when he was little. Lots littler 'n us. When he let people call him Danny. Like as little as Bobby." That concept appeared to stretch the bounds of her imagination. "Then she stopped."

"Aunt Trudi said Gramps is a mean old man with no manners or style and no one in their right mind would want anything to do with him. Mommy should've broken off with him completely like she and Mother—that's what Aunt Trudi calls our Grandma—did."

Lizzie's shift between an entirely different tone and her usual sweetness gave Bexley confidence in the girl's reporting, a fair idea of their Aunt Trudi's voice, and a disinclination to make the woman's acquaintance.

Back to her own voice, Lizzie said, "Mommy made a funny sound like she'd tried to laugh but then she had to cough. Then she looked at us and they stopped talking. Remember, Molly?"

"Course I remember. I also remember when Daddy said Mommy should take us to see her father because family's family and Mommy got real angry and told him to leave the children to her and she'd leave the cows to him. And you weren't even there then."

Molly turned to Bexley. "Mommy never brought us to see him. We met him when Mommy died. He was sitting way in back at the funeral and Daddy led all of us to where he was and said to say hello to our grandfather. So we did. But he didn't say much and we didn't see him again until now."

Her matter-of-fact tone didn't change when she added, "I'm warm enough now to take off my jacket. Cleaning's hard work, isn't it?"

They all set back to work, while Lizzie took Bobby to the newly cleaned women's room.

"I potty like Dan," the little boy bragged. His older brother turned bright red.

Bexley hid a grin and said an internal thank you to not have that issue to deal with.

Dan finished the light bulbs as Kiernan and Eric completed cobweb duty. Without being asked, the three males started on the floor in the open middle area, while Lizzie joined her sister, washing and drying glasses in the sink, while Bexley dusted, washed, and dried the unimpressive assortment of liquor bottles.

"How in heaven's name did you let this get to such a state?" Pauline demanded of Gramps, now that her toils took her—and her trash bin—to the bar's end closer to him. "It must have been a functioning establishment at some point."

"Wasn't no establishment, it was a bar. Plain and simple. Folks came in, had a drink—"

"Played some pool." In response to several curious looks, Kiernan added, "Marks on the floor. Size of a pool table. Light would have been directly over the table."

"Yeah, plenty of pool played here," Gramps said.

"What happened to the table?" Kiernan asked.

"Broke down a while back. Eventually, I burned it."

"Burned it?" Kiernan repeated. "In that stove? It works? Burns wood?"

"What else would it burn?"

"This whole place if it doesn't work right," Kiernan replied promptly.

"Nah. Outer walls and foundation's rock."

"Great," Dan said sarcastically. "Foundation and outer walls will survive, inside'll go up with us in it."

"Listen you—"

Kiernan spoke over Gramps. "Both of the restrooms are short on lightbulbs. How about taking care of that next, Dan."

"Sure. Glad to get away from my lowlife grandfather."

"I'll lowlife you, you—"

"Go," Kiernan ordered Dan.

Eric stepped into the line of sight between the boy and the grand-father. Pauline did more. She squared off to Gramps.

"Quiet."

They all obeyed and resumed their work. Except Gramps, who got out of his chair, deposited sleeping Bobby in a nest of the bags by the doorway, and clumped out of the bar area.

Bexley stood on her favorite stool again to clean the inside of the windows. It was hard to tell how much good it did. The outside of the windows was thickly encrusted and the little visible past the dirt consisted of dense movement.

She climbed down and took glasses the girls had washed and dried and began returning them to the lowest of the cleaned shelves between the windows.

After a few minutes, Bexley said quietly to the girls, "Gramps is your grandfather?"

"Uh-huh. Daddy said he was Mommy's daddy."

Bexley's lips parted.

A small motion caught her attention. She shifted her gaze slightly. To Kiernan. He and Eric had shifted to cleaning the tables and chairs and they set them up in the open area. He looked back at her and shook his head almost imperceptibly.

Don't ask her.

It came as clearly as if he'd spoken.

Bexley licked her parted lips, an instinctive delaying tactic. Except Kiernan's gaze followed the motion and another instinct threatened to kick in.

She cut it off, replaying Lizzie's words in her mind. Reacting to the uncertainty in the girl's voice, Bexley said, "Then he is your grandfather. You have two grandfathers—your mom's father and your dad's father."

"Oh, Daddy's father died a long, long, long time ago," Molly said. "Even before we were born. And his mother, too. So we never met them. We didn't meet this grandfather for a long time, either. But we've met Mommy's mother."

Not an experience of unalloyed joy, judging from her tone.

Handing glasses to Bexley, Molly went on.

"She said she'd met us when we were little babies, just born. She said that a lot, about how she held us. But we only remember her coming a couple times, and then when Mommy died."

Bexley felt a burning under her collarbone, as if she'd run a longer distance than she ever had before. But she kept all her focus on the little girl whose mother was dead.

Molly wrinkled her nose. Fighting tears?

"She smelled. Just like Aunt Trudi, except even worse. Daddy says she takes a bath in something that makes her smell that way, while Aunt Trudi takes a shower in it."

Not tears, but remembrance of an over-scented woman.

"We wouldn't be here now, if Daddy had any other choice." That echo of her father's words might or might not mean she understood the implications for their finances. "Because Mommy isn't here to look after us anymore. She's in heaven."

Molly looked into Bexley's face, gauging. "That's what we're supposed to say. Grandma told us we're not supposed to say she's dead. We're not supposed to call her Grandma, either. We're supposed to call her Mimi, even though it's not her name. And Mommy *is* dead."

"I'm so sorry, Molly and Lizzie."

Molly's thin shoulders relaxed slightly, possibly because she hadn't been called to account for deviating from *Mimi's* script.

Bexley would be tempted to call the woman Grandma, or maybe Granny, as often and loudly as she could.

"I miss her."

"We miss her," Lizzie said softly.

"Of course you do. Both of you. All of you."

From the other side of the bar, Pauline said loudly, "We appear to be done with the cleaning at last. I believe it's time for lunch."

CHAPTER EIGHT

They all headed for the store.

When Bexley would have passed Kiernan in the doorway, he turned, then stepped sideways, partly into her path, taking hold of her elbow so they were side by side, headed opposite directions.

In a low voice, he said, "Let her—them—come to you. Let them tell you what they want to tell you. Don't press them with questions. Let it come from them."

"I—" She'd intended to say I *wasn't going to*. But she *would* have asked. If not for him shaking his head.

Without saying more, she nodded.

He gave a brusque nod back and released her elbow to enter the store.

Looking around to check on where the kids had gotten to, she saw Pauline had watched the exchange, though she was not close enough to have heard the words. A sheen of speculation crossed the older woman's brown eyes.

Bexley could have told her she was barking up the entirely wrong tree.

But acknowledging the speculation might invite more. Better to ignore it.

She ducked her head and joined the girls in checking out the offerings in the cooler.

Lunch was not going to be a high nutrition affair.

"Bexley, can you help me heat this up?" Molly had a reheatable and pre-packaged hot dog.

Dan had nachos and dip. Lizzie held macaroni and cheese that matched the fluorescent orange of Dan's choice. Bobby had a handful of bubblegum.

Taking this all in, Pauline said, "After this meal, you will not be free-ranging. And you, young man," she added to Bobby, "are coming with me now to find something else."

Bexley led the way to the microwave by the coffeemaker. Beyond them was a door with a "Private. Strictly private. Stay out." sign. That must be where Gramps disappeared to, since he wasn't in the store and he certainly hadn't gone outside.

She'd heated the hot dog and bun for Molly, who added chips to her meal, and had almost finished Lizzie's nuclear-glow mac and cheese when the "Private. Strictly Private. Stay Out." door jerked open.

Bexley caught sight of a hallway before Gramps emerged and shut the door with enough emphasis to barely land this side of a slam.

"More raiding of my store, I suppose," he said.

Before anyone else responded, Pauline called out, "Of course. How else are we going to eat?"

"You could pay for it, you know. Cash register still works."

She scoffed with a sound, then returned her attention to the little boy. "Look at this nice apple, Bobby."

Gramps clumped to behind the counter, looking out the window, and fiddling with something producing a lot of static sound.

Bexley helped the girls take their food back to a table set up under the wagon wheel light, then returned to the store for something for herself.

Kiernan and Eric were talking in low voices near the front of the store.

Bexley caught Pauline's eye, raised an eyebrow toward them. Pauline shrugged slightly.

Dan finished at the microwave and headed for the bar room.

"We're going to need to figure out better food choices for those kids," Bexley said to Pauline.

"Yes. Along with a number of other logistics. Food, shelter, warmth, cleanliness—"

"—and distraction."

"Indeed. Here, Bobby, you carry the apple, and I'll bring your soup and milk." In an aside to Bexley, she said, "The milk won't last much longer."

Bexley checked over the limited fresh produce—three more apples, a dozen oranges, wilting lettuce, two carrots, an onion, and eight bananas quickly going soft. She took one orange and a soup heatable in its container.

While she waited for the ancient microwave, she called home. "Mom, it's Bexley."

"Bexley! How are you? Wait—Don't say anything yet. I'm putting you on speaker. Okay. Go ahead. We're all here."

A flurry of hellos followed before she could get back to her reason for the call. She explained the unexpected weather.

"Oh, we know. The Curricks called and told us about your text that you didn't even get out of Wyoming," Mom said.

Dad added, "We found it on the map." He did love his maps. "You're somewhere safe and warm?"

She thought of the restrooms, the chilly bar room, the propane, the dubious food choices. "I'm fine."

"What about the people you're with?" Mom asked with a certain pointedness. "Are they all … nice?"

Uh-oh. What had the Curricks said?

Quickly, Bexley enthused about the kids, even making Dan sound cherub-like, Pauline, and Eric.

"What about the guy—?" Her younger brother, Matt, broke off— likely under a maternal glare.

With a fair assumption of casualness, Bexley said, "Oh, Kiernan, the guy I was driving with is here, of course. And the store's proprietor."

"How long do you think you'll be there?" Mom asked.

She sighed. "It's not looking good for Christmas, I'm afraid. But I'll get there as soon as I can."

Her other brother, Tim, said with relish, "It depends on how fast the major blizzard moves. It moved in faster than expected, which helped form the pre-storm that caught you, but now it's slowed way, way down. It's basically sitting on top of you, dumping snow."

"Thanks for your enthusiasm," she said dryly.

That started sibling banter making them all feel better.

The microwave finally beeped. "My soup's ready. Better go."

"Call again, as soon as you can, Bexley. Or if you want to talk."

"Thanks, Mom. Love you all."

CHAPTER NINE

As she returned to the bar area, she distributed jackets to the kids and put on her own—without the movement of cleaning, the chill of the room set in hard, even with the warm food.

Eric and Kiernan soon joined them, prompting a pushing together of two tables so they all fit around, centered under the wagon wheel light.

Kiernan brought a sad-looking sandwich and chips. Eric had mac and cheese. "Couldn't resist," he said ruefully when he saw Bexley looking at it. "Comfort food despite the color."

"Where are you all from?" Pauline asked the kids.

"Home," Bobby said brightly.

"That's right."

At Pauline's approval, the little boy held out his arms and leaped from Molly's lap. Pauline caught him with an *Umph*.

She settled him on her lap, looked at Dan, and said, "Anywhere more specific?"

"We have a ranch. Not far from Far Hills."

"South and a little east of Knighton." Eric supplied the detail. "Pauline and I live in Bardville now, but we were heading for Chicago for Christmas."

"Is that where you're from? I'm from Waukesha, Wisconsin. I was supposed to fly into O'Hare then take the train to Milwaukee, and my family would have picked me up." Bexley released a small sigh. "When the flight was canceled, driving seemed like the last shot to get home for Christmas."

"Exactly." Eric smiled at her.

"What he's not telling you—" Pauline's great show of disapproval did not fool anyone. "—is he wasn't trying to get to Chicago for Christmas at all. He was going to stay in Bardville. I was the one who wanted to get back for the holidays. And when the flight was canceled, instead of accepting the inevitable, this fool insisted he drive me."

"Didn't turn out too great, huh?" Eric's smile was full of self-deprecating charm.

Bexley smiled back. "It was worth a try."

"So, you were going to Bexley's family for the holidays, too, Kiernan?" Pauline asked.

"*No—*"

"No." Kiernan's negative came in second but was far calmer. Bexley, without looking in his direction, subsided and let him carry the explanation. "I'm headed for Boston. Actually past Boston—Gloucester, Massachusetts. Wisconsin's, uh, on the way."

"Are you and Eric family?" Molly asked Pauline.

Bexley could have kissed the girl for that diversion.

"Not at all. I work for him."

Eric's voice was dry but affectionate. "Do you? I keep forgetting."

With great dignity, she said, "He's trying to intimate I boss him around. That is not accurate at all. I am his employee."

"What brought you from Chicago to be hired by a Wyoming lawyer?" Kiernan asked.

"I'd worked for him in Illinois. When he left everything and everyone he knew in Illinois to strike out for Wyoming with no plan or connections, I continued my employment with him here."

They all stared at her. The three youngest kids apparently impressed by her extremely dignified manner.

"Uh, you do know it undercuts your claim that you're merely Eric's employee when you moved halfway across the country to continue working for him?" Bexley asked.

Eric's snort expressed agreement and amusement.

"Good jobs aren't always available for women of my age." Her stiff dignity melted under a glint in her eyes. "Besides, it was time for an adventure. You get stuck in your ways if you don't try something different."

"*This* isn't the kind of adventure any of us had in mind," Eric said.

Kiernan huffed an agreement "The radio said the storm's earlier, bigger, and slower than predicted. Look, we're going to be in this room for the duration. We'd best assess our resources. We need more heat. If we can get wood to burn in the stove—"

He broke off.

They all followed the direction of his gaze.

Gramps stood in the doorway like a harbinger of doom.

"The *real* storm's coming in now. It'll go the next thirty-six hours, easy."

The sound of the wind *was* fiercer. And whether it was the power of suggestion or reality, it suddenly felt chillier.

Bexley looked toward Kiernan. He was looking at her. She raised her eyebrows slightly and flicked a look toward the kids.

"Whatever the propane supply, you need to expend some to heat up this room," Kiernan said, his gaze on Gramps.

"Could have all the propane in the world. Wouldn't matter. This room's only got the two vents on the wall with the store."

"Then we'd best find wood to get this stove going. We can break up the tables and chairs if needed."

"Break up my tables and chairs? You're crazy. You're not—"

Kiernan overrode him. "You're confident the stove works? Won't send smoke or fumes back in here?"

"Can't guarantee nothing's built a nest up the flue or such. But you're not breaking up anything—"

"We'll do what needs doing."

"Then haul the wood in. But if you're going to do it, you better get to it. There's not going to be less snow any time soon."

They all stared at him.

Eric asked, "*What* wood?"

"The firewood out front the store."

"You have—? Of all the wrong-headed dunderheads—No. Not wasting time on that now." Though Pauline's tone indicated she might devote time to the matter later. "Where?"

"Told you—out front the store."

"Under the tarps," Kiernan muttered.

"Yeah. And now under the snow."

CHAPTER TEN

He and Eric were already up, putting on their jackets. Dan also stood, pulling on his, though it was noticeably thinner. The men exchanged a quick look.

Kiernan said, "We'll run it as a relay. Each of us handing off to the next one. Me outside."

"And me," Eric said.

"Dan, will you take the door? Then, we'll pass it in as far as we can. Might need to do another relay to get it to the stove."

Faster than Bexley could have believed, they had it set up. Kiernan and Eric outside, shoveling off the snow already weighing down the tarps atop two mounds of firewood, battling the wind that buffeted every step. Dan, at the door, had more protection. Next came Bexley and Pauline, but even being in the store, they were hit by blasts. The girls stayed around a corner, between shelves, but insisted on helping, though they took turns tracking Bobby, who was zipping up and down aisles, then into the bar room.

Gramps appeared prepared to sit it out, until Lizzie dropped a log. He grumbled his way up out of a chair and stomped over to her, picking up that log and another coming along and took them to the stack inside the bar room.

And he stayed on as the last stop on the relay.

They worked fast, all of them panting with the exertion and the icy air hitting their lungs. Kiernan and Eric took the brunt and Bexley felt relief when—the last log transported down the line—they could both finally get back inside. They stamped their feet, how much to shake off the snow and how much to restore sensation she didn't know.

They didn't take off their jackets.

No one did.

With all the cold that had come in, it was only nominally warmer inside, but at least the walls cut the wind and the roof held off the snow.

They set up another relay to get a few logs to the other side of the room, but this pace was almost leisurely. Plus, she and Pauline conspired to set Kiernan and Eric to dealing with the actual fire-starting—less strenuous and hopefully warm sooner.

Eric tested the chimney first by lighting a roll of newspapers then held up the stack.

Bexley craned to see if the smoke would go up or U-turn back into the room, which would indicate an obstruction.

When Eric said, "Not perfect, but seems good enough," she thought she heard several exhalations.

"It's plenty good," Gramps said. "How do you think we heated the bar all those years?"

His contention was proved after Kiernan and Eric got a good fire going and they all began to steam slightly.

The mood turned downright giddy when they were able to take off their jackets.

Kiernan asked Gramps, "Is there more firewood beyond what you had in front?"

"Got some in a shed, but it's old. And it might as well be in Montana for the chances of you two fellas getting to it and bringing it back in this storm."

"How far away is this shed?" Eric asked.

"Quarter mile."

"What use is firewood a quarter mile away?" Dan scoffed.

"It was of use when I got a real good deal on it—free—when the bar was running and I used up a lot of wood each winter. Had so much wood at one point, I was stashing it everywhere."

"Then you used up what was closer, until now all you've got is too far away to be of use." Dan sounded far too old and world-weary for his years.

"Yup." The old man was unrepentant. "And if you burn these

chairs and sit on the floor—"

"Not going to sit on this floor, despite our cleaning," Pauline declared. "No, we can't burn the chairs, but we can disassemble the old shelving units in the store and burn the wood."

Gramps squawked in outrage.

Pauline smiled slyly, and everyone joined her, even Dan.

"Before we get to the chairs—or the shelves—there was wood in that storeroom where we checked the propane connection. Broken furniture and scrap," Eric said.

"Those are my projects. A bit of fixing and those things'll be good as new."

Dan rolled his eyes, and this time Bexley was tempted to join him.

"Whatever is burned in it, we need to keep Bobby away from this stove," Pauline said.

"He knows *hot*," Molly said.

" 'Ot," he repeated. "Ow."

"That pretty much covers it." Eric grinned.

Pauline frowned. "The way he runs around he could careen into it by accident."

"What if we make a semicircle of the stools, turned upside down, a distance from the stove? The warmth can get through. But it will be a barrier for Bobby and give us an early warning system."

Before she finished, Kiernan and Eric started moving the stools. They filled in a gap with a table turned on its side.

"What are we going to do now?" Molly asked, her eyes gleaming.

"Now—" Bexley drew out the word as if to extend the anticipation for her audience instead of wondering if she was crazy. "—we begin celebrating Christmas."

CHAPTER ELEVEN

"Christmas?" Gramps repeated in disbelief.

"*Christmas!*" Molly and Lizzie chorused—thrilled, but quiet, as if afraid to believe in it enough to be louder.

"How?" Dan added a sneer to his disbelief.

"Well, let's start with thinking about what we associate with Christmas." Bexley fought for time and prayed for inspiration.

Eric backed her up. "Great idea. Do you know what she means by what we associate with Christmas?" He focused on the girls, but took any pressure off them to answer by saying, "It means what sort of things make you think about Christmas. Like…"

"Reindeer," Pauline contributed. "The North Pole. Wreaths."

Bexley added, "Garlands. Christmas lights. Carolers."

"Snow and cold," Dan said sourly.

A rusty crack of sound emerged from Gramps. "Got plenty of those two."

Feeling the atmosphere slide toward grim, Bexley raised her eyebrows at Kiernan twice in quick succession, prodding him to supply an antidote.

"Goose and ham," he said.

Not what she expected.

Her or anyone else, based on the looks directed at him.

"Goose?" Molly asked.

With the same bewildered intonation, Bexley asked, "Ham?"

"It's traditional Irish Christmas fare—food," he added quickly to resolve the puzzled frowns on the faces of the two little girls. Bobby appeared half asleep and Dan was studiedly uninterested.

"Don't have goose in the store and the only ham's in sandwiches."

Gramps sounded triumphant.

"That's too bad, because it would be nice for Kiernan to have the smells and tastes of his traditional family Christmas, wouldn't it?" Bexley said staunchly.

"What about cookies? They smell and taste good. Would those be okay instead of goose and ham, Kiernan?" Molly asked.

"Cookies also are traditional Christmas fare for my family," he said solemnly.

"Ours, too. Our Mommy bakes cookies at Christmas. She did."

"All year," her sister supplied in a low voice.

Molly nodded. "But even more at Christmas. Lots of special kinds of cookies, but she'd make the very most of Dan's favorite, chocolate chip, because he can eat a *lot* of cookies."

Her emphasis drew faint smiles.

"Well, let's see what we can find in the shop that might let us make cookies. Gramps?" Bexley chose to interpret his growl as an invitation. "Do you have an oven? Not the microwave—" She cut off his response, which he'd telegraphed with a glance in that direction. "—but a real oven."

"Oven? What do you want with an oven?"

"To bake cookies. For Christmas."

"There are bags of cookies or boxes you can buy. Don't need any oven."

"Store-bought cookies aren't right for Christmas," Molly told him. "You have to make them yourself. That's what Mommy said."

Judging the girl had sufficiently cowed Gramps, Bexley followed up with, "Do you have an oven?"

"Course I got an oven. Indoor plumbing, too."

"Wouldn't bring up the subject of plumbing, if I were you. Touches too closely on the state of the facilities," Kiernan muttered.

Pauline, apparently not hearing Kiernan, still proved his point. "Good heavens, I hope it's not in the same state as the restrooms."

"Doesn't matter what state my oven's in. You're not using it."

"But we *have* to have cookies for Christmas." Molly stared at him. Her twin's part of the double whammy might have been even more powerful, because tears came into her eyes as she, too, looked up at him.

"Coo-kay," Bobbie added in plaintive appeal.

"Fine. Go ahead. Use it. You might blow us all up, though. Don't know the last time the propane connection was checked, because I'm no fancy man needs all that sort of fussing."

"Cookies," Pauline declared with the gravitas appropriate to matters of State, "are not fussing. We'll check the propane connection first, then we shall consider what ingredients this establishment offers for the making of cookies. Come along."

Everyone followed her, with Gramps bringing up the rear.

Finding herself next to Kiernan, Bexley murmured, "Do you know anything about propane tanks?"

"Enough to blow one up."

She side-eyed him and decided he was kidding. She hoped.

They trooped back through the store to the door marked "Private. Strictly private. Stay out."

As Pauline reached for the knob, Gramps said triumphantly, "It's locked."

The knob turned under her hand. With admirable restraint, she limited herself to a quick, satisfied glance at him.

He began grumbling about hordes of people piling in on him, not letting a man catch his breath, much less take his usual precautions. But then he needed his breath to keep up as they all moved along a short hallway, then into a bedroom made dim by the storm outside. Pauline flipped the wall switch and surprised them all.

The room was neat and clean. The wide bed was made, with a quilt smoothed over the surface and the pillows plumped. A large recliner displayed worn spots on the arms and seat, but appeared clean and displayed a carefully folded throw on its back. A table lamp and small table with books on it sat between the bed and the recliner. Across from it, a medium-sized television showed minimal dust. The dresser next to it was just as clear.

Pauline, who had stopped two feet into the room, pivoted and leveled an accusatory look at Gramps.

Lizzie gave voice to the woman's expression, shorn of the accusation. "You can clean!"

"Why didn't you do this in the restrooms?" Eric asked.

Looking at his feet, the shopkeeper said into his beard, "Told you. Don't want people piling into them."

Kiernan appeared to be having trouble keeping a straight face.

"Well—" Pauline propped her hands on her hips. "—this resolves one question. The girls, Bexley, and I will sleep here, with Bobby, and we'll make up beds for you boys in the bar."

"Not me," Gramps protested. "I'm sleeping in my bed. The rest of you can make do with sleeping bags and…"

He had to hurry to catch up, because Pauline had started forward again, ignoring him.

"Not there," he shouted as she opened one door.

It was to a bathroom. With their varying heights and some maneuvering, everyone could see it matched the bedroom for cleanliness and order.

Pauline harumphed.

Gramps grumbled, but didn't look up.

The tiny kitchen was also clean and orderly, though Bexley guessed disuse explained it here, in contrast to the bedroom and bathroom.

Gramps rallied. "You'd best all get out of here in case the propane blows if you *really* want to test it," he said with relish.

Dan scoffed, "We'd smell it long before that."

"Right. Rotten eggs, isn't it?" Kiernan asked.

"Or skunk," Eric said, while Dan nodded.

"Fine, fine, but the lot of you back up so I can get to the oven to turn it on. Not you," Gramps said sharply as Pauline reached toward the oven. "My oven. If it does blow, it'll be me. Even if you all did force me to my death."

"No, no. Don't do it," Lizzie said.

Gramps looked down at her in surprise. She'd caught the side hem of his loose jeans in one fist. His expression changed. Gruffly, he said, "Don't you worry. I'm too tough to get blown up by a stove. Now, go on, all of you. There's not room in here."

That was true.

Dan took Bobby from Molly and flopped in the recliner. They took up less than half of its width.

"C'mon, girls, let's go see about ingredients," Bexley urged them. "This is one recipe I know by heart."

CHAPTER TWELVE

The girls found frozen cookie dough right away, a clearly unnecessary fallback option as they gathered butter, sugar, flour, eggs, even baking soda—though in a rather dusty box.

"But no chocolate chips," Molly pointed out. She carried the mini-carton of eggs, while Bexley held the other ingredients in a pouch created by holding out the bottom hem of her large sweater.

"That's okay. Have you ever had M&M cookies?" Bexley led them into the candy aisle. "We can use those instead of chocolate chips."

They didn't greet her suggestion with as much enthusiasm as she might have hoped.

"But chocolate chip's Dan's favorite," Lizzie protested.

Her sister nodded. "And if we can make him chocolate chip cookies, maybe he won't be so sad this Christmas."

The top of Bexley's nose prickled with threatening tears. She doubted cookies would cure the boy's heartache, but making them for him might help his sisters.

"Okay. Then, we'll make our own chocolate chips."

"Can you do that?" Molly regarded her with wide eyes.

"Sure. After all, what are chocolate chips but chips of chocolate? So, we'll chip chocolate."

Lizzie pounced on several plain chocolate bars. Her hand hovered over more. "What about some with nuts?"

"Great idea, Lizzie."

The girl added those to Bexley's sweater pouch.

As they prepared to return to the private area, Pauline, Kiernan, Eric, and Gramps emerged, Pauline holding a finger to her lips. "Those boys are sound asleep."

"Bobby missed his nap yesterday and Dan was up real early with Daddy, loading the truck."

Bexley thought of the man, who'd probably been up even earlier and now was out in this storm. She sent up a good thought for him and returned to what she could do something about—making his kids' Christmas a little brighter.

"We're better off mixing the dough out here, anyway," Pauline said. "Since this man doesn't have a mixer and the kitchen's so tiny we'd be on top of each other. I found this pot we can use for a bowl, a measuring cup, and three stout spoons. I also found—" Pauline added with emphasis. "—that the man has a set of real dishes. No more paper plates."

"Paper plates don't need washin'."

Pauline majestically ignored Gramps' complaint.

At the table, the girls took turns proudly unloading the ingredients from Bexley's sweater.

"No vanilla," Bexley told Pauline.

"Ah, but a bit of brandy will do. And I saw some in the bedroom."

"*What?* Now you want my brandy? What next?" From outraged, Gramps' expression turned crafty. "Besides, you shouldn't be giving alcohol to kids."

"A couple of teaspoons divided among all the cookies will be okay, not to mention baking will remove enough of the alcohol."

"Then what's the point?"

Kiernan and Eric received disapproving looks from Pauline for their poorly masked chuckles at Gramps' retort. Bexley escaped because she was behind Pauline when she grinned.

"Flavor is the point. Go get the bottle. And don't wake up those boys."

That settled, Bexley tackled the next improvisation required.

"Kiernan, Eric, can you find a hammer or something else to pound with and be our designated chip makers?"

"We also might need some brawn for mixing by hand," Pauline said.

"Sure, but what are you going to put them on to bake?" Kiernan asked.

"I don't suppose there was a cookie sheet?" Bexley looked to Pauline.

"I didn't see one, but maybe—" She tipped her head toward Gramps, coming toward them with a slow, reluctant tread with the bottle cradled in the crook of one arm.

Pauline took it from him without waiting for him to offer it. "Thank you. Do you have a cookie sheet?"

"A—? No. Never had any need of such a thing."

"Baking pans? Glass pans?" Bexley asked.

Pauline and Gramps shook their heads simultaneously. Odd to see such unison in those disparate characters.

"I did see a couple skillets," Pauline said.

"My cast iron skillets? They belonged to my granddad," Gramps objected.

"Then they're not likely to be hurt by being in the oven. But even using both, they wouldn't hold many cookies at a time."

"One big cookie," Eric suggested. "Then we could cut it up. Like a pizza."

"Pizza… Wait a minute, in college we used to rewarm pizza in the cardboard box in the oven," Bexley said.

Kiernan backed her. "Of course. We did the same thing. There must be cardboard boxes around here we can break down."

"Won't a cardboard box burn?" Eric asked.

"Not a'tall," Kiernan said. "One of my roommates' father was a fireman and he said it doesn't burn until four-hundred-and-twenty-something degrees Fahrenheit. Unless cookies—"

"Three-fifty, maybe three-seventy-five. But the cookies will stick unless—aluminum foil. We need aluminum foil."

Gramps reared back as if Bexley had slapped him. "Aluminum foil? I don't have aluminum foil in my kitch—"

"It's in the store. I saw it on the shelves," Lizzie said.

Bexley patted her shoulder. "Good eye, Lizzie."

"My store? My store? Again? Who's going to pay for all this coming out of my store?"

"You are," Pauline said. "For your grandchildren to make and eat Christmas cookies."

Gramps glowered and continued muttering under his breath, but he did not contradict Pauline, nor did he try to stop his granddaughter from scooting into the store and returning with a roll of aluminum foil held aloft as triumphantly as the Olympic torch.

CHAPTER THIRTEEN

While Pauline and Bexley guided the girls in measuring and combining the initial ingredients, Kiernan and Eric pounded away at the candy bars with a hammer and the handle of a huge screwdriver they found behind the store's counter.

The guys also were a huge help in stirring the chips into the thickening batter.

They found suitably stiff, corrugated cardboard and cut it to cookie-sheet-sized dimensions, which Pauline and Bexley covered in aluminum foil.

"Looks like we might need another box to be safe," Pauline said.

Kiernan stood. "Saw one in the store. I'll get it."

On impulse, Bexley followed.

She caught up with him where the back aisle intersected with the one that led to the front door.

"Kiernan."

He turned, surprised.

So was she, because they'd practically collided.

"Something wrong?"

"No. Yes. Just… We *are* giving these kids a Christmas."

"What?"

She checked over her shoulder. Yes, they were being watched from the other room.

She got a grip on the loose material of his shirt above his elbow and tugged. Although her brain registered she probably couldn't have moved him if he hadn't cooperated, another part of her felt great satisfaction at the idea she'd dragged him down the aisle that led to the front of the store, then into one of the side aisles.

She was not thinking about another time she'd gotten a grip on one of his shirts, how she'd used that grip, and what it led to.

Was. Not.

"I said, we *are* giving these kids a Christmas. You said not to promise them what I—we—can't deliver and I'm telling you we are going to deliver. We—all of us—are going to do whatever we can to make this a real holiday for them." She looked around at hanging rows of beef and turkey jerky packages surrounding them. "We don't have a lot of raw material to work with, so we'll improvise. Somehow. You are going to help, along with Pauline and Eric, because together we can accomplish more for the kids. And there are some things that will be easier for you to do." She waved a hand toward him, carefully not looking closely at what she was waving at. "Strong things. Tall things. You and Eric, I mean."

Back to staring at jerky packages, she cleared her throat and went on quickly. Yanking the bandage off to get it over with.

"Look, we probably could have ignored, uh, what happened last summer if we'd been able to keep driving. Me sleeping while you drove, you sleeping while I drove. We wouldn't have had to talk much at all. But here, now, and with making a Christmas for these kids, that makes it a lot harder. So I'll say it right out to set your mind at ease. I got the message. I won't try to jump you or—"

"You won't?"

"No." She made it absolutely firm, because there'd been something deeper, beneath his quirk of amusement—*with* her, not *at* her. "Or make things uncomfortable for you. For either of us. It was a mistake, you recognized first, and now we're past it."

"Bexley—"

"Don't argue with me. What matters is those kids—all of them. Even if Dan does act like he's fourteen going on ninety-four. We're going to give them a Christmas. It will take all—"

"Okay."

"—of us to—What?"

"I said—" Something flickered across his eyes, as if a grin lurked somewhere. "—okay. Where do you want me to start? Go out in the storm and cut down a tree?"

"Did you see a good tree when we came in? I didn't but, if you saw one…."

She went quickly to the front of the store. Not to get away from a grin lurking in his eyes or anything else to do with Kiernan McCrea, but simply because she needed to look out the window, since the door was plastered over with signs.

With shelves up against the outer wall and the window set high, it required standing on her tiptoes, peering between still more signs half peeled off the window, and trying to see out into the wind-driven snow. But she did it.

Which revealed a flaw in her approach.

After all, even if she could see past the wind-driven snow, she was looking at the parking area. A most unlikely spot for a Christmas tree candidate.

"Didn't see one coming in."

The way Kiernan said his first word sounded more like *dinna* and sent a small shiver up her backbone.

The next instant, she realized more than a word might have started that shiver. Because he'd come up behind her, slightly to her left, and the exhalation of his breath stirred the hairs at the back of her neck.

She clapped her hand to the spot.

That didn't help because now his breath teased the hairs on her arm. She'd swear even his inhalations whispered to them, firing goose bumps across her skin.

"I was concentrating on getting that vehicle through the snow, not searching for potential Christmas trees. Sorry to disappoint you. Do you see any now?"

His words were as bad in the hair-tickling department.

She stepped to the side. Away from him. "See any what?"

"Trees, o' course."

Had his accent thickened or was she imagining it? Didn't matter. Stick to the point.

What was the point?

Oh. Right.

Trees.

She focused outside. Or she tried to. Her sidestep had put the edge of the door and the door jamb directly in her line of sight. Her peripheral vision amounted to a blur of white movement.

He'd go out in this to try to find a tree? To cut it down and haul it—?

"Do you know how to cut down a tree, Kiernan?"

"Whack at the trunk with something sharp. Doesn't strike me as very technical." He came near to saying *someting* and *doesna* and *verra*.

She would not let his accent get to her. She would not.

She turned to him.

And then there was *him* getting to her. The broad shoulders. The sad eyes that should be happy. The darned scent of him, which she hadn't forgotten.

She should have. She really should have.

She backed up. Right into the edge of the counter. Boomeranged into him—full frontal contact. Well, almost. More like her full front into his three-quarters front. His arm and hip and thigh…

Clothed. All clothed. And she was, too, so what was the big deal?

Nothing.

No big deal.

She scuttled sideways, back toward the interior of the store.

Because cold came through the door.

Only because of the cold.

"Have you done it?" Her voice scratched and broke. She looked away so she wouldn't have to see he'd heard the break and divined its cause … *knew* its cause.

"Done … it?"

"Chopped down a tree." Her words came breathless. Because she'd hurried them out. That's all. "Ever chopped down a tree." She spoke as carefully as Eliza Doolittle once she learned precipitation limited itself to flat areas of Spain.

"No. I've not done that."

"A blizzard's no time to start. We'll think of something else for a tree. In the meantime, after we finish the cookies, we'll set them all to making decorations. We'll figure out where to hang them later."

"Bexley?" Lizzie's voice floated to them before she turned into the aisle where they stood. She looked from one to the other of them. "What are you doing? It's cold here."

Bexley turned the little girl around. "It *is* cold here. Let's get away from the door. Do you need something?"

She meant the words for the girl, but they tangled with another meaning when she looked over her shoulder to shoot Kiernan a warning look. A look to remind him not to give away their Christmas plans to Lizzie or the other kids.

No specific plans yet, but they planned to make plans.

As if that weren't convoluted enough, shooting that warning look over her shoulder at him at the same time she said the words *Do you need something?* gave them an entirely different meaning and directed them at him.

And then—and *then*—she imagined the answer was yes and—

Nope. Not going there. Not. Making. That. Mistake. Again.

"Pauline says we need you and Kiernan," Lizzie said.

Bexley stalled for time for her brain to re-engage with a neutral "Uh-huh."

"Because you and Kiernan are the cardboard cookie sheet experts. That's what she said. We have the cookies on them, but she won't let anybody move them in case they bend and the cookies fall off."

CHAPTER FOURTEEN

Pauline had a good point about cookies potentially falling off.

Kiernan solved the issue by flattening six-pack carriers for beer bottles and sliding them under the "cookie sheets." The six-pack carriers were stiff enough to stabilize, though they couldn't go in the oven because of the colored print and special finish on them.

Even so, the loaded cookie sheets required careful handling to avoid disastrous bends or folds on the first trip to the kitchen.

Bexley stayed behind when the others took that trip.

When they returned, Dan came with. Pauline reported a successful transfer of the first cookies into the oven and Bobby had slept through the commotion.

"I haven't been idle, either. I found instructions on how to make decorations online," Bexley said.

A sort of growl came from Gramps.

"Oh, c'mon, you can't object to us making decorations," Bexley said.

"Should be saving that phone of yours for connecting to better things."

Her smile stalled. "You think the connection will go out?"

"Probably first thing to go. Power next." Apparently satisfied he had all their attention, he added, "Could run out of propane, too."

Lizzie's lower lip trembled. Molly's mouth opened in dismay. Dan scowled fiercely. The adults didn't react as strongly, but Bexley suspected her expression resembled the thoughtfulness she saw in Pauline's, Eric's, and Kiernan's faces.

Kiernan spoke first. "What *is* the propane situation? Should we not use it to bake cookies?"

"Baking cookies won't take much." Gramps' sudden earnestness drew suspicious looks. "Just don't want to waste it."

Bexley bit the inside of her cheeks that he didn't consider cookies a waste. Clever of Kiernan to use that to get an accurate assessment of their primary heat source.

"What uses up the most propane—hot water heater, furnace?" The way Eric asked, Bexley suspected he already knew the answer.

"Hot water. Especially laundry stuff."

"Okay, so we don't do laundry. If we spread out the showers so it doesn't have to work hard for lots of on-call hot water, that should help. Supplement the heat with the wood stove…"

"Then we can bake lots of cookies," Molly declared, dismay forgotten.

No one argued.

But that settled only one possible issue.

Clearly that was on Kiernan's mind, too. "There's naught we can do if the electricity goes out—"

"Keep our phones charged in the meantime," Eric said.

"Good. Have candles at hand. And stockpile what wood we can for the stove against the boiler going bust."

"What's a boiler?" Molly asked.

"It's like a furnace. Or like the stove in the corner we'd best keep stoked."

Part of Bexley's brain was still stuck on how Kiernan's accent turned *There's naught we can do* into something lovely, seducing—No. No seducing. Absolutely not. Not even of her ears.

Besides, there wasn't even a free bed, much less privacy—No. *No.*

"No, what, Bexley?"

She blinked back to the reality of Lizzie's innocent question and the realization she'd spoken one of her *Nos* aloud. "No, we shouldn't use our phones unless we absolutely have to. I already called my family and the Curricks—" She ordered her eyes not to shift toward Kiernan. "—about what happened, that we're safe, but stuck."

"We called to let my hosts in Chicago know I wouldn't be there before you two arrived." Pauline stood. "There's the timer on the cookies. No. You all stay here. I think this is a one-person job."

"We don't have phones, so we can't text. We can't afford them." Molly spoke with a cheerfulness Bexley doubted Dan shared, judging by his sour expression, or that the girls would feel in a few years.

"I'll call my family, then no more calls," Kiernan said. "Or connecting to the Internet. Trying, anyway. Even if we stay connected, calling and surfing take more power. We'll keep our phones charged and not use them unless we must. Agreed?"

The others nodded.

"Agreed. Though I already did some Internet surfing so there's no sense not using what I learned." Bexley focused on the two girls. "But the first project I didn't need the Internet for, because I did it as a child. Do you know how to make snowflakes?"

Their eyes widened. "No."

"All we need is some paper and scissors."

Bexley turned toward Gramps and so did Molly and Lizzie.

"What? What do you want from me now?"

"Paper and scissors."

"What for?"

"To make snowflakes."

"Ain't got enough o' those by looking out a window?"

"We can't see any of those snowflakes," Lizzie said. "The windows are too high."

"And covered over. Besides these snowflakes won't melt," Molly added.

"Aw, hell." He levered himself out of his chair. "I don't know where I've got scissors. Little kids shouldn't be using them anyway. They'll get all cut up."

"I'll watch them." Bexley winked at the girls as they all followed in the wake of his grumbles.

"Suppose you want white paper, too. Don't know I've got any of that. Not like I'm writing poetry 'n such."

"Oh! We can make multi-colored snowflakes," Molly said.

And that's what they did. White on one side and multi-colored on the other from colored flyers and throwaway advertisements.

"You fold the paper over, then over again, and again." Bexley demonstrated. "As many times as you want. And then each cut you make shows up over and over. The more times you fold and the more cuts, the lacier it will be."

"I want to do it."

Gramps found one pair of scissors in a jar of pens behind the checkout counter for Molly.

When the rest of them started toward the bar room, Kiernan remained in the store area, saying he'd look for candles.

Bexley dashed back for one more piece of paper she'd see on a bulletin board over the microwave. If it wasn't stained…

Kiernan was near the front, talking on his phone, presumably to his family.

She snagged the paper. As she turned to go, the sound of the storm swelled and he raised his voice over it.

"Uh-huh. Freak storm. Before the main event. … Safe enough. … What? Oh. They did? … Yes. She's fine, too." His voice picked up speed. "In fact, there's a group here. Four kids, who—"

Bexley cut off the rest with a quick return to the bar room.

Kiernan returned with two large candles and a dozen tea lights, plus a lighter. He put them on the work area behind the bar.

Pauline brought back a plate of cookies and reported she put in the next round.

Bexley used an oversized pair of scissors she'd seen behind the bar. Lizzie wielded a pair of nail scissors Bexley contributed from her toiletries kit like a surgeon, creating delicate paper lace.

Everyone tried a cookie. Gramps had three. Dan ate four.

CHAPTER FIFTEEN

Molly's snowflakes reminded Bexley of her childhood attempts, while her own—thanks to the clunky scissors, of course—resembled something an uncoordinated giant might have created.

While they made these masterpieces, Kiernan and Eric, with assistance from Dan and supervision by Pauline, strung a wire over the bar.

"Do you want this any higher, Bexley?" Eric asked from his position standing on a stool to reach the ceiling at one end of the bar. Kiernan held the same position at the other end.

"That looks good where it is. How're you guys doing up there?"

"It's craic," Kiernan muttered, adjusting his stance on the stool's uneven seat.

Molly assessed him with a clear look and said what several of the adults might have been thinking. "You talk funny sometimes."

"I don't," he said with false indignation.

"Yes, you do." Lizzie broke it to him gently. "Like when you said boiler instead of furnace. And whatever you said just now."

"Craic?"

"What does that mean?" Molly asked.

"Fun, I suppose. Good times."

The girl frowned. "You didn't really mean that, huh?"

He was saved from answering when Lizzie asked a different question. "Do you use weird words because you're from that place near Boston? Where you were trying to get to for Christmas."

"Gloucester? Ah, some from Gloucester do speak in an amusing way. They're particularly haphazard with their 'r's', drop them here, add them there. Perhaps I have picked up a bit in the years I've lived there."

Bexley shook her head. "It's the brogue."

"Brogue is it? I've naught, woman."

The girls giggled at his broad pronunciations.

Pauline said, "It's because he came from a place called Ireland."

"Is that near Massachew—whatever?"

"No. Massachusetts is another state in the United States of America, like Wyoming is. Ireland is a separate country across the Atlantic Ocean."

The girls' eyes widened identically. Molly asked the questions. "You're from another country? Don't you want to go there for Christmas? How did you get here? What's it like being from another country? Are there ranches in Ireland? Do you have horses and dogs and cows there? What—?"

"Hold up. Take a breath, if you want any answers a'tall. I came here from Ireland to go to college and because my older brother had moved here, and I've stayed on, so now I'm a citizen as well. As for Christmas, no, I don't go back to Ireland, because my mother moved here shortly after I did, so Gloucester is where we'd all be together, along with more who are my family now. How I got here? By an airplane. Quite boring, I know."

"Not to me," Dan muttered.

"Indeed there are horses and dogs and cows there. You're more apt to hear them called a farm or a lodge than a ranch, though, and they're considerably smaller than what you're familiar with."

"That's weird they have different names for things."

"There are lots of words for familiar things. Words from all over the world," Kiernan said.

"And lots of folks who live here now came from someplace else," Bexley added. "Or their parents or grandparents did."

"Your great-great-grandmother was from Ireland."

Gramps' words were so abrupt and so unexpected, they all turned to look at him.

"County Mayo. That's where my grandmother was born. And my grandfather was the first of his family born here. Before that, all born in Ireland. My dad's line had some Irish, too. So'd your grandmother's people. We've got enough sprinkled in here and there, probably more than half."

"We're Irish?" Molly asked wide-eyed.

Dan said, impatiently, "We're Americans. It's where you're born and where you live. The rest is just history."

"It's interesting to know the history," Bexley said. "To find out about the people who made decisions—like coming here from far away—that contributed to what your life's like now. Our country has people who came here from all over the world. Sometimes people like to remember, so they'll say they're Italian-American or Swedish-American, Irish-American or—"

"Native American," Molly said. "But they were already here."

"Where's Daddy from?" Lizzie asked.

The adults all looked toward Gramps.

"Don't know about his family." His rough voice said he didn't much care, either.

"He's from Wyoming," Dan said firmly. "Just like us. And our mom. What happened before that doesn't matter."

"I like it," Molly said determinedly. She tipped her head, testing out the next words. "I'm Irish."

Her brother started to speak again, and she said, "Irish-American." She shifted her focus to Kiernan. "Does that mean I can say words funny like you do?"

Bexley leaned toward her. "You better not, or some people will think you're from Massachusetts."

Lizzie and Molly giggled and began re-applying their scissors.

With the wire strung over the bar, the others cut wire of varying lengths and attached individual snowflakes to them, then hooked the opposite end over the cross wire.

But Molly wasn't done with her questions. "Where does the name Bexley come from? Is that from another country? I never heard anybody called that before."

"You don't know anybody," Dan muttered, loud enough to be heard from behind the bar.

"Do, too. I know the kids at school and from when we used to go to church and from town."

"Wow, what? A couple dozen?"

"And I've read lots of names—"

Recognizing a sibling battlefront brewing, Bexley intervened while she still could. "Bexley's the name of where I was born, Molly."

"Where is Bexley? I never heard of it."

Giving Eric a grateful look for backing up her diversion, she said, "It's near Columbus, Ohio. My dad was finishing a master's degree at Ohio State and he and Mom drove to Bexley to pick up a check for yard work he'd done for people there to supplement their income. He did that and Mom worked two jobs as long as she could because they were poor students. They were only supposed to be there for a few minutes, long enough to pick up the check, then get back to campus."

Eric said, "So if you'd arrived earlier or a little later, you'd have been Columbus?"

Everyone chuckled. Even Gramps.

What caught Bexley's attention was Kiernan's chuckle. She felt a hitch of surprise at him joining in with this reaction to her story.

No time to examine that if she was going to keep Molly and Dan from starting again.

"The couple Dad had done the yard work for were terrific. Took Mom right inside, called 911, and I was born in their front hallway. Mom and Dad thought about naming me after them, but which one when they were both wonderful? And their last name was Gunderhausen, so I'm glad they weren't *that* grateful."

Molly and Lizzie giggled as they continued to cut out snowflakes.

"I used to remind myself being named Bexley dodged not only the Gunderhausen bullet, but a couple others. Before I came a couple weeks early, Mom and Dad planned to be back in Wisconsin before I was born. If I had been born in Wisconsin, when I was scheduled to be, I could have been Baraboo."

"Baraboo?" Lizzie repeated, laughing.

Molly asked, "What would they have called you? Bare? Boo?"

Bexley squeezed her eyes shut. "I can't even imagine. Think of what the kids in school could have done with Baraboo. And *that's* not even the worst. Mom and Dad had planned to go for a couple days to a lake in Wisconsin when they got back, as a break before I was supposed to arrive. Mom always said later she couldn't imagine what she was thinking, planning to go to a lake so close to her due date."

"Oh, no," Lizzie said. "The lake must have an *awful* name."

"Well, if they named me after the lake I might have been called Winnie. Because the name of the lake is Winnebago. We used to go there when I was a kid."

Pauline said, "You could have been Van," producing another spurt of amusement.

But Gramps said loudly, "Winnie's a nice name."

The momentary hush as everyone absorbed Gramps sticking up for someone—at least for a name—was broken by Molly. "Gramps, did you know someone named Winnie?"

From the corner of her eye, Bexley thought she caught heightened interest from Pauline.

Above his beard, Gramps' cheeks reddened. "Maybe I did and maybe I didn't."

"Who is Winnie, Gramps?" Bexley asked it gently, though she half expected to hear it had been the name of his favorite dog. Or, considering what his personality said about what kind of pet he might have had, his favorite porcupine.

"Best damn waitress this bar ever had."

"Waitress," she repeated.

"Server, bartender, drink-slinger, whatever the heck you young people call it these days. She was the best. Made folks feel at home. But not mushy. Sharp—her tongue and her mind. Worked here seventeen years. When she passed on ... Well, it wasn't worth the trouble keeping the place running."

"How long ago was that?"

He scrunched up his face. "Must be nearly ten years or so."

Did that explain the state of the place ... and the bathrooms? "Were you and Winnie...?"

"What? *No.* Don't go thinking such stuff. I had more'n my fill with the girls' mother. After she took them and left, I got to have the girls for a few weeks each summer and sometimes other times when their mother wanted to be free of them. Those were good years. Only Trudi got to be an age when she wanted boyfriends and parties, not fishing and dancing parties with neighbors in a little bar by a gas pump. She went crying to her mother and there was a set-to, judge 'n all, and her sister—" He jerked his head toward the girls. "—Angie turned against me, too."

Bexley said, "That must have been difficult."

"Yeah, well. It happens."

He wasn't as inured to it as he'd like others to think or he wouldn't still be so hurt by it.

"But you must have seen Angie again."

"What makes you think that?"

"Dan named you Gramps."

"Oh, that. There were a few years there when she and Hall brought him to see me for a day now and then, and have me down to the ranch to Christmas dinner." He slanted a look toward her, then away. "Hall Quick's doin'. Notions of what's right and due a father. Angie... She wasn't the girl she'd been. When she started having kids, it wasn't like they say some women get sad and depressed after babies. It was more like she'd created a world by having those babies and she didn't want anybody else in it. Not me and not even Hall."

He jerked as if someone stuck a rod in his ribs. Or as if he suddenly realized he'd been sharing his thoughts and feelings.

The girls watched wide-eyed. Dan scowled.

Gramps resumed. "None of that's here nor there. Water under the dam and dried up in the desert."

For an instant, Bexley's gaze met Kiernan's.

She yanked her thoughts back to Gramps, still looking awkward, and—strictly to relieve the older man's discomfort—she took back the reins of the conversation as she delivered more snowflakes to the wire hangers. "I would have been proud to be named Winnie."

"Really?" Kiernan doubted.

"Well, once I was grown up I would have been. But I never would have gotten over the other name they could have chosen if they named me for where we stayed when we went to Lake Winnebago."

Lizzie's eyes widened. "What would you have been named?"

Bexley looked from face to face, drawing out the suspense.

"Buttes des Morts."

"Huh?" came in a chorus.

Bexley printed the three words on a scrap of paper. It was passed from hand to hand.

"That's not what you said," Molly objected. "This says *Butts des Morts*." She enunciated each letter.

"I gave it the French pronunciation because that's what the French fur traders called it when they first came through the area. Or, I should say it's the Wisconsin version of the French pronunciation, because the place has been Wisconsin a lot longer than it was French."

Dan, the last to receive the scrap of paper, frowned at it. "Buttes of the Dead?"

She nodded at his translation. "That's right, Dan. You could say Butte or Hill. Hill of the Dead. They were referring to burial mounds Indians had there for a long, long time." In the spirit of the season, she skipped the story about a conflict between French fur traders and members of the Fox tribe in the 1730s that added another historical layer to the name.

"Your parents wouldn't really have named you Hill of the Dead, would they?" Lizzie asked.

"I don't know," Bexley said with an exaggerated long face. "After all, they condemned me to a lifetime of saying *Bexley, not Becky*."

CHAPTER SIXTEEN

"We've filled up this wire," Eric announced.

"Ohhhh," the girls breathed in unison. The snowflakes twirled from white to colors and back, fluttering between the chill of the windows and the warmth of the stove.

"But what will we do with the other snowflakes?"

"Don't worry, Molly. We've got more decorating to do. We'll use those snowflakes. And the stars we're going to make next."

"Stars?"

"Yes. And since Kiernan and Eric and Dan are done, they can make them, too."

"I hear Pauline in the kitchen—"

But before Eric could accompany his words with a departure to assist with taking out and putting in more cookies, Dan beat him to the doorway. "I'll help her. Check on Bobby, too."

His sisters dented his play for Brother of the Year by gaping at his departing back.

Eric grinned and followed after the teenager. "Maybe there'll be a spare cookie for me."

Reclaiming the attention of her helpers, Bexley instructed, "First, we need more paper. Gramps will help you."

"I'm not—"

"Or you can go without him and bring back whatever you find."

He levered up out of his chair, muttering.

With them gone, she reached across the table, sweeping the cutaway bits into piles. Kiernan's hand came into her field of vision, pushing a pile from his part of the table.

"That's quite a story about your name."

"Thanks." She didn't look up. "It's the truth. If it bothers you—?"

"Bothers me? Not a'tall. Why would that be bothering me?"

Her mouth opened, then closed. "No reason." She gathered the piles into one.

"You plan to throw that out? Hold on to it. Might be of use."

Bexley looked down at the colored bits of paper, then up and right into Kiernan's face that for no reason at all made her chest ache.

"Good idea, Kiernan. I'm not sure exactly what we'll use it for, but you're right. There might be something."

"Confetti," he said with a glint in those green eyes that had a lot to do with her chest aching. "We can use it to celebrate if we're still here for New Year's. Eve."

New Year's Eve.

Midnight.

Kiss.

She looked away.

"Don't even kid about that. It would be a nightmare."

Kiernan watched Bexley making another star.

Why would that be bothering me?

No reason.

For all she'd denied it, there was a reason she'd thought the history of her name would bother him. He couldn't imagine the reason, but she could.

"Next, turn it over and fold that triangle back to the top side. That's right, Lizzie. Good, Molly. Turn it over again—"

"Hold up," Eric said. "I'm a couple folds behind."

Lizzie reached over and helped him catch up.

Bexley had led them through two previous stars, remembering what she'd seen on a video.

Her hands moved deftly, quickly, yet now and then slowing down for a stroke across the surface of the paper, as if she were fond of it. As she had—

Something poked into his side.

He looked over and down. It was Molly's elbow.

"You're not folding." He looked into the girl's accusatory disapproval. "You're just staring at Bexley."

"Watching how she's making the stars," he protested.

"No, you're not or you'd be *making* a star," the other twin tormentor announced.

"I *am* making a star."

"Not a very good one." Surprisingly, that came from Dan, who'd returned with Eric, Pauline, and another plate of cookies.

"Hey," Kiernan objected.

The girls giggled. Pauline, Eric, and Bexley grinned. Even Dan's mouth turned up.

"You'll have to put that one on the back of tree," Dan said.

Kiernan felt Bexley's gaze instantly come to him. He shifted so their eyes met and held.

We have to get these kids a tree.

I know. Ideas?

Not yet. But we'll come up with something.

Then she broke the look and he knew she'd tripped on the concept of *we.*

No reason that should bother him. Though, in reality, they were a *we.* Temporary, of course. As long as this trip lasted. Was supposed to be one long day of driving. Extended now for who knew how long— through Christmas Day more than likely. Perhaps the following day as well.

Beyond that?

Well, they couldn't stay here forever. Wouldn't stay here.

"That was your ornaments Mommy put on the back of the tree," Molly told her brother. "She kept ours on the front."

"Yeah, along with Bobby's red finger-painting blob. It was just pity made her hang those decorations."

"Enough." Pauline's sternness earned obedience, though Molly huffed in outrage.

"I'm hungry," Lizzie said abruptly. "Are we going to have dinner?"

"Yeah," Dan said.

"Fine. We'll finish these after dinner," Bexley said. "Not potluck this time."

"Pot-what?"

"Salad first and then pizza."

That drew the first overt enthusiasm from Dan. "Pizza—all right."

CHAPTER SEVENTEEN

Five months and two days ago

Bexley had never before in her life tumbled into bed.

Not figuratively. And not literally.

Who knew how limbs and hands and skin and shoulders and bellies could tangle, glide, connect and reconnect in the glorious moments of a tumble.

Removing clothes wasn't quite as glorious, but it provided other benefits. Like getting naked. Fast.

Between kisses and dispatching her top and bra, she panted, "This is… crazy."

He *mmm*'d agreement as his mouth covered her nipple. She arched with the sensation.

"Too soon," he ground out as he levered his hips up to let her pull down his underwear.

"Way too soon." She kissed flesh she'd just exposed and he held her head to keep her from going lower.

"It's been a while," he said.

"Me, too."

By some miracle, he found the protection he hadn't needed since—

And then his mind lost that thread, his mind lost every thread as she shifted against him.

He tore the wrapper.

There was nothing elegant, nothing practiced about this. There was the drive, the want, the need.

Inside her, he stilled. His hands holding her hips, hers on top of his, as if to deepen the hold.

For a suspended instant they looked at each other.

Their bodies didn't allow any longer. They were moving.

Fast.

Way, way too fast.

"Sorry." His throat felt raw getting the words out. "Not going to last. Give you the time you need—Not going to last."

"Oh, yes, you will."

And, sputtering between laughter and pain, he did.

Kiernan rolled off her where he'd collapsed, flinging the arm away from her wide as he went on his back, his other arm under her back.

How her body held together when she didn't have a single bone left, Bexley couldn't imagine.

She didn't work at imagining it, because her brain was blank.

He slid his arm free and got out of bed. She moved her eyes to watch him go into the bathroom. Then tracked his return, because that was all the movement she could manage.

He opened the drawer beside the bed and took out another condom.

She groaned. "I don't have a single working muscle left."

He put one knee on the bed. Giving her an interesting and interested angle on his putting on the condom. But only academically interested, because, truly, boneless. No muscles operable.

She couldn't even move to cover herself.

That surprised her. She'd certainly covered herself in that last year and more of Nigel. When you love someone, you believe what they say, verbally or otherwise. Even—or maybe especially—when it's something bad about yourself.

Fine time for insights.

Especially when she couldn't even muster the muscles to protect herself now.

"Sorry. I can't possibly."

Repeating her earlier words, he grinned down at her.

"Oh, yes, you can."

And she did.

Later, much later, they ate cookies in bed from the stash Dave kept in a desk drawer the way old detectives kept whiskey.

She wore one of his t-shirts. He didn't bother with clothes, but kept the covers up to his lap to avoid crumbs.

"You've a piece of cookie, there on your cheek," he told her.

She brushed at the cheek closer to him.

"Other side."

She brushed there but felt nothing.

"Closer to your mouth."

She reached up again, but he caught her hand before it made contact.

Instead, he leaned over and took the crumb from the corner of her mouth, making her nerve-endings shiver. Then he took her mouth.

Coming up for air, he tossed the cookies he still held onto the bedside table past her. She heard a couple fall to the floor, and didn't care.

"You have far too many clothes on. Need to fix that."

"I'm a little chilly," she said with a flicker of a grin.

"We can fix that, too."

With his hands free of cookies, he used one to hold the V of the shirt's neck so low the edges rode across her breasts, while his other hand gathered in the extra fabric at the hem, twisting it around and around to draw it up on her abdomen, drawing his knuckles and the back of his hand against her skin, his touch leaving sparklers in its wake.

The rising hand met the lowering hand, which took hold of all the material under her breasts.

She drew in a sharp breath. He kissed her quick and hard, then backed up enough to look down at what he'd revealed.

His free hand drew one side down over the edge of her shoulder. He shifted his other hand, stretching the V wide. So wide, any movement—from him, from her would slide the material off her breasts completely.

"Your skin's so soft, so white." He rested his hand on her upper arm, where a line showed she had picked up a bit of tan in her time at the Slash-C.

"I hadn't been in the sun at all since last summer."

She'd barely started to reach for him—more an intention than a movement.

The continuation of her movement slid her arm away from his hold.

He stilled abruptly.

Did he misunderstand? Think she'd meant to pull away, when it was an accidental side effect?

She leaned forward and kissed him softly on his cheek, trying without words to say she was still here with him, in this moment, in this bed.

He went from still to stiff.

"Kiernan?"

He opened his hands, releasing the shirt, swung away, his back against the headboard, not looking at her. As if she weren't even in the same room, much less in this bed with him.

Not again.

She knew this distance.

She knew this diminishment.

Never again.

She scrambled out of the bed, feeling the mattress dip as she pushed off it. Holding the stretched t-shirt to her chest, she yanked up her jeans one-handed, crammed her feet into still-tied shoes.

Vaguely, she was aware of stirring behind her.

"Bexley…"

His voice trailed her.

But she was already gone.

Matty and Dave sat side by side on their darkened back porch, watching the stars tickle the Big Horn Mountains, his arm around her shoulders, her head in the angle of his neck.

Until Bexley Farber came flying out of the ranch office, holding her jeans up with one hand and adjusting an oversized t-shirt with the other.

Matty sat up, watching the younger woman.

"Problem?" Dave asked his wife.

"Not one you need to deal with. They'll have to sort this out themselves. I wasn't sure when Val brought it up, but looks like she's right. There might be something to this."

"Wasn't Bexley heading the wrong direction for there to be something going on with her and Kiernan? Not that I'm against it, mind. I'm all for Kiernan getting past the Felicity mess from last summer."

"Hmm. I don't know."

She was quiet so long he felt his eyelids getting heavy.

"Dave—Dave?" She nudged him to full alertness. "When you and Jack and Kiernan went to the courthouse in Jefferson last week, did you take him anywhere special?"

From drowsy, he came fully awake.

"Special?"

She put a hand up to his cheek, as if consoling him for being easy to see through—or listen through. At least for her.

"Flower Power, the shop across from the courthouse?"

He looked down at her, though it was too dark to see details of her expression. "I guess we did."

"What did she say?"

"She?"

"Dave," she warned.

This would be like feeding gasoline to a fire to her matchmaking, but he didn't mind.

"She tried to get Kiernan to buy some flowers. Pasque flowers. He wasn't interested. She tried a little harder and he left the shop, said he'd wait for us in the truck."

"Oh."

Then she didn't say more. Thinking.

"Want to hear what she told him before he walked out?" His assumption of innocence wouldn't fool a defense attorney, much less a wife.

She thunked his arm. "Of course I do, you big lug."

He chuckled. "She told him that after a long, hard winter, pasque flowers are the first to bloom in Wyoming. Course Jack and I knew that. Cheerful little things, see 'em sticking out of the snow sometimes."

"Did you tell Kiernan that?"

"Might have mentioned it. Along with getting your wedding bouquet of Indian Paintbrush at the shop, and a few, uh, interesting encounters there."

"How'd he react?"

"Not interested. I'm not sure he even heard what we said."

Another silence filled with thoughts. "Sometimes winter comes in July. I think there's a lot of reason to hope."

He ducked his head and kissed her thoroughly, with her complete cooperation. "You should have been Mrs. Noah, putting everybody two by two."

"No. I should be Mrs. Dave Currick."

He raised his head, miming being deeply struck by her point. Then he laughed. "Damn straight, Mrs. C."

But Matty remained thoughtful. "It will take time, though. Kiernan's not the only one rebounding from a mess last summer. Val's doing her best to help Bexley, but… Yes, I think it will take time. You know Bexley's ex hurt her…"

He cursed. "He hit her? If he ever comes near her again…"

Matty kissed his cheek gently. "Never hit her that I know of. But there are all kinds of abuse. There's the inability to see the other succeed. When that's dished up by the one who's supposed to be your champion, that can be real hard to recover from. Slow, methodical, mean-spirited tearing down of confidence that comes from a shriveled heart." She tipped her head. "Likely something else shriveled, too."

He shuddered.

Then he invited her inside to their bed for a demonstration that no such calamity had befallen them.

CHAPTER EIGHTEEN

December 23

Dinner wiped out the salad makings and put a major dent in the pizza supply. Remembering a childhood treat, Bexley split the bananas, sprinkled them with brown sugar and lemon, then broiled them, serving them with dollops of vanilla pudding for dessert.

By that time Bobby was yawning so wide and so hard, he practically fell over.

Molly and Lizzie prepared him for bed with the ease of practice, tucking him into a corner of the oversized recliner in their grandfather's bedroom, which they would share with him later.

The good reception for tonight's meal didn't hide that the intersection of nutrition and what the kids liked dwindled from here.

Pauline put it in words as they did the minimal cleanup around the microwave. "We can make more cookies, but real food…"

"I know. We're going to need to think outside of the box."

"But first we have to build a box," she said grimly.

"What if—?"

"Bexley? Pauline?" Molly called from the bar room. "We need your help. Will you come here?"

They entered to sounds of a dispute, though that didn't wipe out Bexley's moment of pleasure at the threshold to take in how much the atmosphere had improved from when they arrived.

The room clean and lit and warm. Everyone gathered around two tables in the center, satisfied from dinner.

"Don't you think we need more decorations?" Molly demanded of the two women the second she spotted them. "Lots more decorations so it'll really be Christmas."

Her grandfather argued, "You already got those stars and snow-flakes you been making all afternoon. They're all over the place."

Molly rolled her eyes in a fair imitation of her brother. "We've hardly got *any*. We need *lots* more decorations. There's nothing in the store or the bedroom or the kitchen or the—"

"Let's hold off on decorating everywhere," Bexley warned. "We're spending most of our time here, together, so let's concentrate on this area."

The girl gave in after a moment's thought. Sort of. "But even in here it's not really decorated."

"It's clean," Pauline said. "That's a start."

Bexley looked around. The snowflakes on the wire were fun. The stars made so far gathered on the bar top for now, waiting a place to be hung. The spray-painted paper trees were still in the store. Beyond that, zip.

Molly had a point.

She turned to Gramps. "You have no holiday decorations at all?"

"Does it look like I've tricked this place out with frou-frou bits and pieces?"

Pauline answered, "Doesn't look like you've made any effort at all for several decades. That, however, doesn't mean you don't possess decorations. Perhaps from some past time."

A shadow passed over the portion of Gramps' face visible above the overgrown beard.

Bexley quickly turned to see if Pauline had caught it. She had. Her just-give-me-the-Christmas-decorations expression didn't change, but her sharp eyes intensified.

"Could be something in the attic," he muttered.

"How do we access the attic?" Pauline demanded.

"Ladder through a door in the ceiling of the back room."

"Where do we find the ladder?"

Eric muttered, "Why do I think *we* is going to be *me*?"

It didn't ruffle Pauline in the least. "You, along with Kiernan, right after Gramps tells you where the ladder is."

Gramps stamped ahead of them, revealing the back room was the tiny storeroom behind the kitchen. Bexley had joined them. Kiernan came last, following her.

As Gramps turned to leave them to it, she put a hand on his arm. "Your grandchildren will appreciate this."

"They're not interested in being my grandchildren. And I'm not interested, either," he added hurriedly.

"Don't be so sure," Bexley said, leaving it unclear which side of the equation she meant. "What Dan said about the car rolling over the curb meaning there was no excitement here?"

"Smart-mouthed kid."

"Not exactly national news. How'd he know what happened?" An arrested look came into Gramps' eyes. "He must be interested enough to keep track of what happens here."

"Huh." With that neutral grunt, Gramps walked away.

"Impressive, Bexley," Eric said.

"I just wish it would do some good."

"It might. Let it sink in."

She smiled slightly.

Kiernan liked that smile. Wasn't so wild about Eric giving it to her.

"I'll get out of your way now," she said, and left.

The back room was so small, the ladder to reach the push-up ceiling door to the attic extended into the kitchen.

With the attic door up, Eric Larkin's torso disappeared into the space above. Miracle of miracles, the wall switch they'd flipped had brought on a solitary bulb.

Cold gushed down on Kiernan like an icy shower as he followed. "What's all that about warm air rising? It's freezing up here."

From in front of him, Eric grunted in sympathetic agreement as he left the ladder for the beams providing what flooring there was in the attic. "Think in this case, the warm air keeps rising through this sieve-like roof and into the outdoors. Also, it looks like the boxes are down at the other end and we'll need to thread these beams to get there."

"I'd go back for gloves if I didn't fear being snared into something worse by those two dictators." Instead, Kiernan followed the other man into the attic space.

"Pauline and Bexley? Or Molly and Lizzie?"

"Take your pick."

"Pauline's orders are why I'm up here. She's supposed to be my employee, but you'd never know it. You and Bexley?" Eric asked, in the vague language of males, which Kiernan knew had nothing to do with whether he and Bexley were connected by employment.

It was another connection altogether Eric Larkin had in mind.

An instant and automatic denial that there was any such connection between him and Bexley or any other female rose in him. Then slammed into the recognition of why Eric asked such a question. The other man was interested in Bexley as a man is interested in a woman. Yet, he wouldn't intrude if Kiernan said yes, he and Bexley were … whatever.

But if Kiernan said no…

"It's complicated."

Eric breathed out through his nose, continuing to edge deeper into the attic. "Isn't it always?"

"Yes. You?"

"Divorced."

Kiernan considered the back of the other man as they carefully moved forward. "Nasty?"

"Not for her. For me it was getting hit in the head from behind with a cement block. After the first blow, it's all a little foggy."

"God, I know how that is."

"Were you married to her?"

"No. Wanted to be. Then it turned out she was only using me." His own words surprised Kiernan. Not because they weren't true, but because he'd said them. Out loud. To a near stranger.

He shifted to the side, following a parallel pair of beams to the ones Eric was on. The pile of boxes almost seemed to retreat before them as they advanced.

Eric neither looked toward him nor asked any questions.

Kiernan added, "Not sure if it's better or worse that it wasn't the run-of-the-mill kind of using. She went after me to get to my brother's wife's cousin's fiancé."

Eric whistled. "Your brother's wife's... Uh..."

I'm her husband's ranch foreman's wife's cousin's husband's brother.

Bexley's delight following the thread of the puzzle. Her laughter. Her nearness. Her touch—

Kiernan shoved aside memories with an abrupt question to Eric. "Why on earth would someone store boxes on the far end of the attic?"

"Perhaps leaving room because he planned to store all the things in the back room up here. Although, considering our host, more likely it was pure cussedness."

"Definitely pure cussedness. Anyway, yeah, it was my brother's wife's cousin's fiancé." This time he held off the memories that rundown sparked. "He'd been a suspect in a murder way back—"

"Jack? Jack Ralston?"

Kiernan stopped and faced him. "Yeah. You know Jack?"

"I do. A little, anyway. Met the Curricks through a lawyers' group, and met Jack through the Curricks. Heard about when he was finally cleared of suspicion. Why'd this woman want to get to Jack?"

"She's the younger sister of the woman he'd been suspected— wrongfully—of murdering. Even with her cousin proved as the murderer, she wasn't ready to let go of blaming Jack."

"But you had no idea of the connection."

"Not the connection, not any of it until she spilled her venom at Jack and Val's wedding after getting me to invite her as my guest."

Eric shook his head. "How'd Bexley react to all this?"

"She wasn't there."

"I mean when you told her. Isn't that why it's complicated between the two of you?"

"I've not told her."

Was that part of what was complicated between them?

Abruptly, his brother's voice came into Kiernan's memory.

You know she's not Felicity...

Whatever you did or stopped doing or how you stopped doing it flicked on her movie in her head.

So it *was* part of it. At least according to Cahill.

Eric pivoted his head, giving him a look all too easy to identify, since it matched the soundtrack of Cahill's words replaying this moment in Kiernan's memory.

It made for uneasy listening.

Eric turned back to the depths of the attic, lighting up the boxes with the flashlight on his phone, stopping at one. "I believe we've found Christmas."

CHAPTER NINETEEN

The girls opened the flaps on the first two boxes, while Kiernan and Eric went back for the other two they'd brought down.

Gramps scowled at their return. "What the hell—? What did you get into up there?"

"The boxes from the attic you told us about," Eric said as he and Kiernan put down the second load of boxes, side by side.

"Not those boxes. Not those. Ones marked Christmas okay, but not those." Gramps tried to gather two of the boxes but they were too bulky for him to corral.

Bexley, Pauline, Molly, and Lizzie all looked around at the agitation in the man's voice.

"That's Mommy's name on that box."

Molly's statement drew Dan's attention. "And Aunt Trudi's. What's in these? Is this Mom's stuff—?"

"They're mine and nobody else's. None of your business what's in them. They're going back in the attic right now."

Apparently recognizing he couldn't maneuver both boxes at once, he took the one marked "Angie," a good tactic from his point of view, since that was the one the kids were reaching for.

"You can't go up that ladder," Kiernan said. "Especially not with a box."

"The hell I can't." Gramps resisted Kiernan's effort to relieve him of the box. Kiernan prevailed.

"We'll put them back. We didn't mean…" Eric trailed off, giving the kids a rueful look. He picked up the other box. "Sorry."

Molly half stood, but Bexley tugged at her hand. And Lizzie inadvertently tugged at her curiosity.

"What's this?" The girl held up a vaguely boot-shaped form.

"Open it up. Take those two ends," Pauline instructed.

The two ends Lizzie held came back together as the paper insides opened into a three-dimensional form.

"It's a bell." Molly sank back down beside the Christmas boxes. "Look, here's another one. Can we hang these up?"

"Sure." Bexley mentally crossed her fingers Gramps didn't react to these the way he had to the boxes with his daughters' names on them.

"What're these?" Molly held up two sad, plastic rounds.

"They go around candlesticks," Pauline said. "Supposed to be poinsettias, I suppose, though they're so faded they look more like those flowers around Bardville that bloomed real early. Pasque flowers, that's the name."

Kiernan's head snapped up.

Before Bexley could wonder much about that, Molly had a new find from the box. "Oh, look. Ornaments for a tree. These are pretty."

Pauline took the wobbly old box with glass ornaments from Lizzie. "We have to be careful with these. They break very easily and could cut you just as easily."

She retrieved two more boxes of ornaments, setting them aside.

"These won't break." Molly came up with a box of candles in the shape of choir boys and girls, snowmen, Christmas trees, and Santas in varied poses—in a chimney, on his own two feet, steering a sleigh.

That hollowed out the first box and they opened the second as the three men returned.

Gramps pulled the chair he'd previously occupied farther away. Eric and Kiernan gave small, *No idea* shrugs in answer to questioning looks from Bexley and Pauline, then joined in withdrawing snarled strands of old Christmas tree lights from the box.

"Oh, boy, we can hang lights," Molly said.

"Not these lights," Kiernan said. "I can see from here the cords are brittle and cracking, those plugs show fraying."

"But—"

"No."

Even Molly recognized that finality and looked back into the box for more treasures.

Boxes of Christmas cards with Currier and Ives scenes drew little interest from the girls, but Bexley put them aside as potentially useful.

A layer of crushed tinsel garlands came next. "We can fluff those up," Bexley said.

A tree stand took up most of the rest of the room, but Lizzie pulled out one more item swathed in yellowed tissue paper, about the size of a loaf of bread.

Peeling back the tissue revealed a green ceramic Christmas tree with tiny multi-colored lights on the ends of its branches.

"I had one of those," Pauline said with a reminiscent smile.

Kiernan reached over and ran the cord through his hand, then examined the plug.

The two girls turned expectant looks to him.

"Maybe. I'll need to check it more thoroughly first."

With that hopeful ending to the explorations, they went off to bed. Bexley went along, but they were self-sufficient, even standing on the upside-down trash can to reach the sink to brush their teeth.

She pushed back a pang at their being so self-sufficient, wished them a good night, and returned to the bar room.

While she'd been gone, the guys gathered sleeping bags and other gear the Curricks had stashed in Kiernan's vehicle and Eric and Pauline had traveled with, along with a few things from Gramps' back room, setting up four sleeping areas in the bar room, clustered near the stove.

"Okay," she said brightly, "now we have to figure out presents."

"Presents? Whaddya think this is? A la-di-da gift shop?"

"No chance of that." Bexley's brisk response drew faint grins from everyone except Gramps.

"At least you have that much sense," he grumbled. "So enough of this malarkey about gifts."

"It's Christmas. Those babies are going to have gifts."

"Like what? Beef jerky?" Dan's cynicism suffered when his voice cracked—not from emotion, but hormones.

"Ain't nothing wrong with jerky," Gramps snapped.

Dan, naturally, rolled his eyes—again. Didn't his eye muscles cramp from doing the same motion over and over? "Gifts are set, then."

"No jerky. C'mon, we'll put our heads together and think of something," Bexley encouraged them.

Silence.

Pauline said, "I have a necklace. Those little girls like jewelry?"

"Can't give something to just one of them," Dan objected.

"You and your grandfather are full of obstacles, aren't you? Ever have constructive ideas?" Neither responded to Pauline's challenge. "All right then. It's a long necklace. We cut it in half, tie the ends together, and there we go, two necklaces."

Bexley beamed at her. "Brilliant. I have some toiletries—not makeup or anything—but a few things little girls might like."

"As do I. We can put something together," Pauline said.

"I gotta knife," Dan drawled. "Which of 'em would want that? Bobby?"

"What kind of knife?" Gramps asked unexpectedly.

Dan scowled. "A knife knife. A sharp edge and—"

"A hunting knife? A Bowie knife? A—"

"Pocket knife."

"Huh."

Dan stared at his grandfather a moment, then jerked his hands up shoulder high, keeping his elbows in. He reminded Bexley of an adolescent bird.

"Huh, what?"

"We'll set to whittling, that's *huh* what."

"Whittling? *Whittling?*"

"Yup. I got wood. I got a knife, you got a knife, that's two knives."

"I can't whittle."

"Not yet, you can't."

"We're saving the wood to burn. Heat, remember? So we don't freeze," Dan said.

"Hard wood's better for burning. Pine'll burn too fast, pop all over, and leave a mess. But it's good for whittling. Cuts real easily. Some say it doesn't give the sharp cuts, but for a beginner that's okay. Course the sap gums up your knife so you're cleaning it a lot and even then it gets on your hands. If you're the kind minds mess, you don't want to try. Sap—"

"I don't mind sap. It's—"

"—or you're afraid of failing—"

"I'm not afraid of—"

"Good. Then we'll get started."

"I don't—"

He gave up, because Gramps had left the room.

They shared a few more ideas. Pauline suggesting scouring the store for items.

"Great. Especially stocking stuffers—Oh. We need stockings." Bexley looked around at the others.

"If we absolutely have to, we could use their actual socks," Pauline said.

Dan said nothing, but his glower deepened. Did none of them have socks to spare? At least clean ones—and with the moratorium on laundry because it used up propane… And then there would be another issue.

"Bobby's would be so small, we wouldn't be able to get anything in it."

"That would solve the whole issue."

Bexley fought a desire to growl at Dan. He was a kid. A kid in difficult circumstances that extended beyond a few days of a storm.

Plus, at that moment, his grandfather stamped back into the room with several pieces of wood and an old knife in a case. Eric rose and offered Gramps the chair next to Dan.

The grandfather nodded his thanks. The grandson did not look the least grateful.

"We'll think about the stockings overnight," Bexley said. "We still need a tree."

"What about the one from the box?" Eric asked. "If Kiernan thinks it's safe to plug in."

"It's good."

"Great. But it's tiny. It's not someplace to put packages under."

Gramps interrupted his low-voiced instructions to Dan to scoff, "Packages." Then he said, "They make a tree by stacking up Jack Daniels' barrels in the town where they make it. That's my kind of tree."

"In the spirit of the season," Kiernan added.

"*Spirit* of the season." Gramps' repeat ended in a croaky sound that had them all turning to him. "Spirits. Because that's what Jack Daniels is."

"Somewhere down in Texas uses deer horns to create a tree," Eric said.

"Using what's at hand," Bexley murmured thoughtfully.

Kiernan nodded. "Gloucester has one from lobster pots and buoys. And I've seen hubcap trees along the highway."

"Okay," she mused, "what do we have lots of?"

"Jerky," Pauline said.

After the chuckles died, she added, "Sorry, Bexley. No ideas about a tree, but I had another idea for presents for the littles. As a teenager, I made yarn octopi for my young cousins. Stuffed animals—sea creatures. I could do them with assistance. If—" Pauline turned to Gramps. "You have yarn?"

"Yarn? What would I be doing with yarn?"

"Knitting, crocheting, or—" Pauline's deadpan turned pointed. "—selling it to those who do."

"Nope. Got twine—"

"A child cannot cuddle with a twine octopus. It will scratch."

"—or baling wire."

Pauline's nostrils flared. "*Baling wire?*"

Apparently unaware of her outrage, Gramps cautioned, "Not a whole lot of it and it's out in the shed, so it would be a rough trip to get it. Besides, I don't know why a kid would want any kind of octopus. Especially a Wyoming kid. It's not like a horse or a dog. Or even a cow or a sheep or a goat. What's the point?"

"The *point* is to give those two girls and their little brother something soft and lovable, unlike their grandfather."

Cutting off Gramps, who finally seemed to recognize Pauline's pique and appeared to be about to reply in kind, Bexley quickly said, "What about fabric? Could you use strips of fabric instead of yarn, Pauline?"

"Fabric. That's … interesting. What were you thinking of?"

"The towels we found behind the bar?"

"They'd need to be washed. Doing it by hand, I doubt they'd dry in time. And the machine…"

Looks pinged around the four of them. Kiernan said what was in the looks. "We shouldn't risk running out of propane to wash old towels. Or to dry them." He looked at Bexley. "Even for a toy for those kids."

"That's right," Gramps said. "Not practical."

Pauline stood. "So, we'll choose from your clean shirts."

"My shirts! You can't take one of my shirts."

"I don't intend to take one of your shirts. I intend to take two."

CHAPTER TWENTY

Pauline stood firm on the number of shirts and she had the initial choice, but agreed he could save some of her choices from their octopi fate … down to the final two.

She went quietly into the bedroom, careful not to wake the three sleeping, and returned with seven shirts.

Squawking that they were brand new, Gramps immediately removed a white and dark blue. Then he dithered and complained until Pauline threatened to make the decision for him. He sacrificed a solid red and a red plaid. "Excellent. This will look Christmassy and you certainly can spare red shirts. That's half your wardrobe."

She instructed Eric and Kiernan on cutting the shirts into narrow fabric strips. Bexley started the hunt for three suitable soft balls to form the octopi heads before Pauline joined her.

They found three play balls that would do.

Gramps limited himself to a groan when he saw the package of balls being opened. Then he resumed instructing Dan.

They cut and sorted the fabric, but before they could do more, yawning became epidemic. They bundled up the fabric and stashed it away.

Dan was in his bedroll and asleep before Bexley and Pauline left the bar room.

He should be as sound asleep as the other three men nearby.

Instead, Kiernan, on his back, with his hands tucked under his neck, stared at the decidedly uninspiring ceiling, replaying the day … and avoiding any replays from farther back.

That didn't keep his memories from getting him in trouble.

Have you done it?

She'd said those words and he'd flashed back to when he had.

Of course, he had—*they* had. Their bodies hot and slick and awkward and so right.

How could she ask? She knew. He knew she knew. For all that she pretended he was a pesky piece of furniture in her way every time she turned around.

He'd not felt like a piece of furniture standing close behind her, not even when she'd sidestepped to be clear of him. Nothing like a piece of furniture. Especially not when she brushed against him for a bare second—against her wishes, as she made clear by nearly leaping away.

While he… Well. The cold through the store's door was all that let him recover soon enough to not make a total *amadán* of himself.

He listened to the wind knocking at the building, a faint scratching sound when it picked up a drift of snow and flung it at the walls.

What were the chances of Pauline bringing up the same flowers the woman at that place Dave and Jack took him had gone on and on about? She'd acted like they had significance to him, when he'd never heard of them before. What had she said? Something about they could be toxic when fresh, but medicinal later. How they bloomed so early, they promised spring, even in the snow.

Then, louder than the storm outside, a little girl's voice sounded in his head.

You're not folding. You're just staring at Bexley.

He hoped to hell he could still say he hadn't made a total *amadán* of himself when this was all over.

CHAPTER TWENTY-ONE

Molly and Lizzie didn't need sugar for a sugar high.

The excitement of Christmas Eve day was more than sufficient.

And Bobby caught the contagion. He ran in circles, flopping on the floor, jumping up, and repeating whatever either of the girls said.

After a short consultation, she and Pauline dug into the store's stash of eggs for a protein-heavy breakfast.

It gave the three youngest more endurance to bounce off the walls.

The storm also seemed to have gathered force overnight. It drove a fine mist of snow around the edges of the store's door.

The small bedroom had been warm enough with the girls and Bobby sharing the huge chair, while she and Pauline had the bed. Body heat also helped out the stove when they were all in the bar room, but Bexley passed through the store at double-time when it was her turn to use Gramps' bathroom.

She showered in record time, too, twisted her hair around, then up, pinning it at the crown, leaving the ends wild and free.

It wasn't great, but with limited hot water, it would have to do.

In her suitcase for a change of clothes, she spotted her traditional Christmas pajamas in a corner of her suitcase and let out a sigh.

Traditional as in a family tradition. All the Farbers had PJs of the same ersatz Scandinavian fabric, with lines of snowflakes, hearts, reindeer, and Christmas trees in white on a red background. If they moved too fast around each other the disjointed lines could make onlookers dizzy.

Their mother started the tradition of family pajamas when they were little.

They outgrew them faster than they wore them out. Until the year Mom gave them these pajamas when they were all grown. Amid the laughter, they'd resolved to wear them every Christmas. Not another night of the year, but always Christmas Eve.

Not this year, though. Not for her.

She picked up her phone, still fully charged, but showing no connection. Sometimes texts went when calls wouldn't.

Still fine. Making Christmas here for 4 kids & the rest. Love and Merry Christmas Eve to all.

"Oh, good, Bexley. I hoped you were here," Pauline greeted her as she left the bathroom for the bedroom. She held up a shirt on a hanger. "What do you think of this?"

Before Bexley could respond, Gramps clomped two steps into the room then stopped dead. "What's that you've got?"

Pauline spoke with total calm. "A red shirt."

"*My* red shirt."

"I figured that, since it was in your closet, though it's not worth hanging in anyone's closet. Look at these cuffs. They're completely worn. So's the collar and placket."

"Plack-what?"

"The front strip where the buttons and buttonholes are. It's frayed all the way down. You can't possibly wear it. But—"

"Sure I can wear it."

"—we could use the fabric. We could make it work for stockings."

"Oh, that's great, Pauline." Both combatants ignored Bexley.

Gramps' scowled deepened. "*Hey.* It works for me as a *shirt.*"

"Does it?" Pauline held up the shirt. It was straight where he turned round. "When was the last time you wore it?"

"I was savin' it."

Pauline propped her hands on her hips. "For what? When you've nearly starved to death and have an urgent desire to wear a shirt down to threads on the cuffs and collar and placket?"

He growled. He grumbled. He folded.

"All right, all right. Take it. You all have taken over everything else. Don't know why you shouldn't take the shirt off my back. Want my undies, too?"

"Decidedly not. This shirt needs brushing and airing before we use it. I'll see to it."

She took the garment, picked up a kit from her suitcase, and went to the kitchen.

As Bexley started past Gramps to head for the bar room, he murmured, "That's a hard woman, that is."

He sounded more impressed than critical. And she could almost swear that somewhere under the messy tangle of beard, he smiled.

CHAPTER TWENTY-TWO

"There." Bexley finished the last squeeze of the scissors and a stocking-shaped piece came free of two taped-together pieces of paper that escaped the snowflake- and star-making efforts of the previous day.

It had taken a couple tries to get a pattern she liked—with plenty of commentary from the girls, even though they were set up at the other end of the two tables, with a project to turn catalog inserts from newspapers into Christmas trees.

It involved folding two pages a time in a large triangle from the top and a small triangle from the bottom. Then tucking those turned pairs back into the spine, leaving their outside parts rounded. Pauline helped Lizzie and Kiernan helped Molly with that part, which required manual dexterity.

In the meantime—under Pauline's remote supervision—Eric carefully secured unbroken ornaments on the windows and wall sconces. All well out of Bobby range.

Bobby sat with his grandfather and Dan by the stove, their backs to the rest of them. Bexley knew Gramps was directing Dan in whittling. Bobby stayed occupied by mimicking them with a bar of soap and his fingernails—they sure would be clean.

It reminded Bexley of her family Christmases when everyone would be wrapping at the same time, secrets happening in each corner of the room, yet all of them together.

Of course, they wouldn't be in a rustic—putting it kindly—bar room. They'd certainly have Christmas music playing in the background and wonderful smells coming from the kitchen.

She'd missed that in her years with Nigel. He'd spent one Christmas with her family, but insisted he couldn't possibly leave New York for the holidays after that.

She hadn't realized how much she'd missed being home until last year, arriving there still raw from the breakup. She sank into the security and comfort and love of home, starting her healing.

This year, her anticipation started building early. She wouldn't be a sodden mess of misery for this holiday season. Not to mention she had an exciting new venture, getting off to a great start, in no small part thanks to Val Trimarco Ralston.

But she would still enjoy home after the storm passed. For now, the point was having as good a Christmas as possible for these kids.

Bexley put aside the templates she'd duplicated the right number of times.

"Now to figure out how to get eight of these to fit on the shirt to make four stockings," she murmured.

"Been meaning to ask, how do you plan to fasten the fronts and backs together?" Pauline asked from the other end of the table. "I have a bit of thread and a needle in my kit, but not enough to sew these."

"I was thinking about that… Gramps—?"

"Don't have no sewing kit." Proving he was listening from over by the stove.

Or was he keyed into Pauline's voice? Bexley felt a smile flicker.

"But if you can't put the fronts and backs together, how will the stockings hold anything from Santa?" Lizzie's worried question reflected in her sister's expression.

"*Och*," Kiernan said to them in an exaggerated way that sounded more like a badly faked Scottish accent than his normal voice. "Have no worries. Doncha know by now Bexley always has another idea and another?"

Molly grinned at his accent.

Lizzie nodded solemnly. "She does, doesn't she?"

"Thanks, Kiernan," Bexley grumbled wryly. "No pressure."

Molly looked at her. "You do have an idea, don't you?"

She held up a wait-a-minute finger. "Gramps, what about a stapler? Do you have one?"

"One of them guns? Might have one of those. But it'd be out in the shed."

He sounded more satisfied than sorry at informing her of that impediment, but Bexley pretended not to notice. "That's okay. Something not so vicious would probably work better."

"A staple gun?" Pauline said, incensed. "You'd tear right through the fabric. Never heard of anything so nonsensical."

Kiernan looked down quickly, but Bexley saw his grin. A chuckle came from Eric, wiring an ornament over the second window. Fine for them to think the squabbling was humorous while she played the peacekeeper…

Okay, she was having trouble suppressing her grin, too.

Dan spoke up. "He's got a couple back-to-school packs in the store that didn't sell. Might have staplers in them. They're on the end of the aisle by the jerky."

"Can't go breaking up those packs. They're sold as a set."

"Haven't sold," his grandson said with equal stubbornness, "and looks like they've been there a lot longer than this fall."

Gramps' *humph* sounded like Dan had that right.

Pleased at the teenager volunteering something to help with their projects, Bexley pushed a bit more. "Terrific, Dan. Would you go get them, please? I think if we staple the stockings, with the staples very close together, then turn them inside out carefully and if Santa doesn't stuff them *too* much or put heavy things in them, they should last at least a day."

She hoped.

She kept that to herself as the girls' faces glowed with the anticipation of stockings stuffed by Santa.

But before they could put that to the test with the stapler Dan brought back from those back-to-school packs, Bexley hit a different snag.

She had two pairs of the patterns on the back, fitting easily when she nested the top of one into the curve of the toe of the other. But she couldn't get the remaining four pieces out of the front material.

Bexley sat back with a sigh. "They're not fitting."

"I don't need one. They're for kids," Dan called, once more seated by the stove.

"You're getting one."

Did he even know what a fraud he was? Working hard over there on a gift for one of his sisters while trying to sound like a world-weary old… Well, actually, a lot like Nigel.

"If only this shirt were bigger," she muttered.

"He'd never have given it up then," Dan said.

"That's the truth," Gramps confirmed.

"If we have to, we could put the side seams down the back of a couple, though we might need to staple those, too, because the seams are coming loose and I'd hate to have the stockings burst open down the back. We could use different material for the backs—"

"*Another* one of my shirts? I'll be goin' naked in another day."

Kiernan cut through Gramps' outrage and the others' sputtering of chuckles. "To avoid that calamity… Mind if I try something, Bexley?"

"Not at all."

She started to get up, to leave him the chair directly in front of the spread-out shirt and the stocking templates.

His hand on her shoulder pressed her back to sitting, while he leaned in from the side.

Close.

Too close.

"What if you put the patterns horizontal on the front, straddling the side seams? Having the seam there makes it look like a cuff." He moved the patterns into position, then flipped back the top of one to show her what he meant. "You can get four on the front that way, then do the up and down pairings on the rest of the back to easily get the remaining four."

"Cuffs—that's perfect. This *will* work."

He turned his head toward her, smiling her enthusiasm.

Close.

Too close.

She tilted away from him and, still, he was too close. Her heart jumped up, battering against her ribs as if it could reach him.

He stepped back.

Relief.

That's what she felt. Relief.

"Do you want me to do the cutting, Bexley? Could be hard going with those old scissors."

She popped up from the chair so he could take it. "Yes, that would be great. Then I can help the girls with the next step on the trees."

CHAPTER TWENTY-THREE

Kiernan cut—more like hacked—through the material with the old scissors—while they took the next step with the two paper-folded trees. They spray painted them green, using cans from the store … which Gramps protested, but without his usual enthusiasm.

Eric helped set up an area for them to spray paint in the store with an old sheet and cardboard.

Then they left them to dry thoroughly.

Bexley, the girls, and Eric hung the paper bells from the ceiling on either side of the wagon wheel light fixture.

"Too bad we don't have mistletoe to hang from it," Pauline said.

Kiernan jerked his head around and saw Bexley and Eric standing together under the wagon wheel, exactly where mistletoe would hang.

"Okay, now we start stapling the stockings," Bexley said cheerfully.

"I'll staple," Eric volunteered.

Were they both as indifferent to mistletoe as they sounded?

"Good. I'll turn them right side out. Girls, you straighten up. Then I have something else for you to do."

As Kiernan looked away from Bexley and back to the cutting of stockings, he found Pauline watching him with a knowing smile.

He knew half an urge to tell her there was nothing to know. Couldn't be. If there'd been any chance it ended in July, but there hadn't been any chance anyway… Because.

But there was no saying that aloud. Denying what she thought would only make it more real.

A whisper in his head pointed out two thought that now—Pauline and Eric.

Didn't matter. He knew otherwise. He and Bexley knew otherwise.

CHAPTER TWENTY-FOUR

Five months and two days ago

"I don't know what I was thinking."

Outside the airport—this was no conversation for eavesdroppers—Kiernan sat on a boulder set in a bed of rocks to call his brother. The discomfort suited his mood. He'd packed up last night, leaving in the still dark, before anyone stirred on the ranch. He left Matty and Dave a note—called away by work, of course.

Why bother being original.

He'd stood at his rental vehicle and looked at the building Bexley occupied.

Then he'd got on with it and drove to the airport.

"Thinking?" his brother scoffed cheerfully. The miracle was he'd figured out Kiernan's meaning from his disjointed phrases. "No thinking involved."

True.

"Who?" Cahill asked.

"You don't know her."

"You've been at the Slash-C."

"You don't know her," he repeated.

"Must've been fast," Cahill said thoughtfully.

Too soon. They both knew it. He was sure they'd both known it. But the need...

His brother asked, "Strong attraction?"

"Attraction?" The waves from her echoing contractions, drawing him deeper. Not like the bracing—ah yes, *bracing*—ocean waves of his native Donegal or his adopted New England. But waves of heat, surrounding him... "Yeah. Into bed nearly straight off."

"Is that so?"

Kiernan grunted fatalistically. "Did you talk to Val or Matty, then?"

"Me? Neither one of the two."

"They talked to Eleanor," Kiernan concluded, which might as well be them talking to his brother. "So you know we were both at the ranch a few days, was all."

"And you were as good as rude to her."

Cahill sounded as if he found that significant. Lifelong experience told Kiernan arguing would be seen as proof of his guilt. He hadn't been truly *rude.*

"Until," Cahill said, "you took the girl to bed one time with no thinking."

Kiernan made a noncommittal sound.

Cahill, proving his interpreting skills, stated, "Ah. Not one time. You had a repeat performance of tumbling, no thinking."

"Not the last time. That was thinking alone. You could say I came to my senses."

There'd been a different tumbling. The tumbling of memories. Chips of memory forming a mosaic of Felicity's betrayal. The simple phrase, *last summer.* An arm pulled from his hold. A final kiss on his cheek.

Last summer. It made all the difference. Confirming she'd used him from the beginning. *Every day. Every touch. Every moment together. Using him.*

"What do I know of this woman—any woman? Very little." He heard *very* come out *verra,* a sign his accent had thickened, a sign— according to Eleanor and Val—of emotions close to the surface. "Nothing."

"You know she's not Felicity," Cahill said calmly.

Kiernan snorted. "I don't. I'm not competent to know that, as I didn't know Felicity wasn't Felicity."

He braced, waiting for Cahill to say he couldn't know *anyone* wasn't Felicity without getting to know the person better and that meant giving the person a chance. Trouble was, giving Bexley a chance meant getting close to her and that meant wanting to make love to her, which opened a can of worms.

Not worms.

Snakes.

Boa constrictors.

"So, that's that? End of this Bexley, eh?"

He was silent too long. "Yes. She was off like a shot, so…"

"What sent her off, then?"

"Don't know."

"You hadn't spoken a word?"

"I hadn't."

His brother's silence demanded more.

"I stopped."

"Stopped…? Uh, in flagrante?"

"In foreplay." Kiernan swallowed. "The third time."

"Ah. So you stopped. And she was off like a shot."

"Why do you say it like that?"

"Like what?"

"Like you're the wise old man on the mountain and I'm the novice come to collect your wisdom."

"Because it's wisdom I've got."

They'd been through this before. Many times. In humor and the comfortable shoulder-shoving competition of brothers. But that was before Felicity. Before Kiernan's failure to see what was happening between them stood in stark contrast to what Cahill had with Eleanor.

"All right, then. Dispense your wisdom, oh, Ancient One."

"I'll give you *Ancient One* and make you suffer when next we're together. But for now I'll show my superior understanding and wisdom. She had her *own* movie playing in her head."

"What?"

"You each have your own movie playing in your heads. The happy news is when you're with the right woman, and there long enough, the movies in your heads are about each other and happy ones. But where you are now, your movie in your head's about Felicity. You said as much. It's what made you stop. You were in the moment with Bexley the first time—excuse me, times—and in foreplay the third. Then something switched on the movie in your head about Felicity. Isn't it?"

A pair of words—*last summer*—with its instant reminder of Felicity. Bexley drawing her arm away from his hold as Felicity had done. Her soft kiss on his cheek.

"Yeah," he said slowly.

"And whatever you did or stopped doing or how you stopped doing it flicked on *her* movie in her head. And that's why she skedaddled out of there."

What was the movie in Bexley Farber's head?

No. He didn't care. He couldn't care.

He'd left the Slash-C before he had to—*had to*—see her again.

He was getting the hell away from her.

Far away. For good.

CHAPTER TWENTY-FIVE

December 24

The stockings were done.

The girls had viewed them with awe when Bexley turned them right side out as if they were gossamer.

Kiernan, aware of Pauline's attention, tried not to watch too closely.

Now Bexley planned a reprise of the star-folding, though she wanted them to use different materials.

"It's a treasure hunt. Find whatever you can that we can fold into more stars, but especially what's red or green or gold or—oh, even better—shiny. Something that sparkles."

"What about alum-uh… alum-num foil like the cookie sheets? That's shiny."

"That's an excellent thought, Molly, but it's so thin, I'm afraid it wouldn't work."

"Over something," Dan murmured. "Not as thick as cardboard."

Bexley's eyes lit up. "Oh, if you could make that work…"

Kiernan pushed down the thought that he'd damn well make it work if he were Dan.

"Come now, let's begin this treasure hunt." Pauline herded them toward the doorway.

Molly stopped there and called back, "Aren't you coming, Bexley?"

"You all go on ahead. I need to think about something."

Kiernan devoted himself to clearing the table, using that as an excuse to stay here.

Gramps didn't bother with subterfuge. He just stayed seated.

Pauline didn't even glance at him, much less try to cajole him.

Kiernan could swear he heard a disgruntled sigh from the older man.

But then he forgot Gramps and concentrated on Bexley's seemingly aimless wandering around the room.

It was hard to track her movements without seeming to. He pivoted to see Bexley give her head a rueful shake and move away from staring at the bar.

She made another circuit of the room, looking intently at nothing he could see. Then, from a position close to the doorway to the store, she turned and stared back across the room, past him and the table, to the opposite wall.

The corners of her lips turned up. Her eyes opened slightly wider. She'd spotted something.

He twisted to look where she was looking, but it told him less than her face did, so he twisted back toward her.

"Hubcaps."

Few people ever spoke that word with the warmth Bexley gave it.

What if she said his name with that dreamy, caressing intonation?

She had. Once. Before—

"What?" His word came out rough.

She didn't seem to notice, still staring at the wall of hubcaps.

"You said they make trees of lobster pots in Gloucester and whiskey barrels or deer antlers in other places."

Cautiously, because he might have an idea where this was going, he acknowledged he had said part of that. "Yeah."

"And hubcaps." She moved across the room to the incomplete display of dulled hubcaps, touching one here, looking up at another, testing the weight of a third. "How do they do that?"

"I've no idea. None a'tall."

"It would need a framework. Say, a cone of chicken wire around a ladder... No, something stiffer, to hold them up..."

"What are you saying over there about my hubcaps?" Gramps demanded from his distant chair.

"If you moved closer and didn't deny yourself the warmth of the stove and the company of your family, you'd know," Bexley called back to him.

Kiernan stood, took a couple steps closer to her.

"With no desire to be the Grinch, I'd point out we've nothing of the sort here. No chicken wire, never mind something stiffer. Not even much more wire than what we used to hang the snowflakes."

She pulled her bottom lip in between her teeth, still looking at the hubcaps. She backed up, nearly stepping into him from not looking where she was going, surveying the hubcaps with her head tilted this way and that.

What on earth did she see when she did that? He tried shifting his head for a different view, but still saw a wall of grimy hubcaps, and not all that clearly, because neither the wagon wheel light fixture hanging from the ceiling, nor the lights behind the bar had much illuminating oomph by the time they reached this wall.

"If we can't have a three-dimensional tree, we might make do with a two-dimensional one," she said at a last.

"Of hubcaps?" He didn't doubt her, not after what she'd created already. But he did wonder how.

"Of course. That's what we have to work with, like those other trees. Antlers and whiskey barrels and lobster pots. We'll have to scrub them all so they're shiny. I like green trees better than shiny, but it will have to do."

He felt something like a ball of lead plunge low in his stomach. He'd cleaned many a hubcap, working part-time at a carwash and detailing business while he was in school. But he'd had all the tools and potions available, not to mention not one of them had started as grimy and dirty as the best of these. Gramps had collected them in the wild, so to speak, mostly straight from dirt roads. Then they'd sat beside the stove for who knew how long, adding smoke to their mix and baking it all on.

With industrial cleaners and a week, they might be able to return the sparkle to that wall of hubcaps.

"Let's start with one, you and me, and see how it cleans up."

She stilled.

He suspected it was the *you and me*.

"You've set all the others to tasks." He spoke casually, as he moved past her, regarding the hubcaps and picking out the least dingy. "Think this one's the best. Agreed?"

"Agreed."

In accepting that as the best candidate, she'd also agreed to them doing the chore together.

He lifted it from the nail it hung on.

"Hey. What're you doing? You'll leave a hole in my display," Gramps shouted as the others trooped back in.

"It looks better already," Pauline said stoutly.

He was quelled into disgruntled mumbles.

Kiernan's feeling of being pleased with himself continued while Bexley *ooh*ed and *ahh*ed over every shiny, colored, reflective bit of paper they'd found, then wrote down the steps in case they forgot how to fold the paper into stars while she was otherwise occupied.

He and Bexley gathered the cleaning supplies they'd used yesterday, adding a stiff brush from the closet, then went into the women's room.

Bexley propped open the door, with a murmur about bringing more warmth into the small space.

It *was* chilly.

But he thought it had more to do with the prospect of being in that small space with him. That left his self-satisfaction as dented as any of the hubcaps.

CHAPTER TWENTY-SIX

After an awkward start, they'd found a good working rhythm.

One-quarter of the circle soaked in the sink, then rotated up to have more cleaning solutions sprayed on it. Kiernan plied the wire brush once it had gone through those first two steps. Then she scrubbed with a cloth to remove what he'd loosened.

Starting on a second go-round of the hubcap, Bexley felt the weight of the silence dragging at her. Surely it couldn't be worse if she started a conversation.

Impulsively, she said, "You're good with those girls. I'd have expected you to be good with Dan, probably Bobby, but, honestly, I'm surprised you're that good with Lizzie and Molly. You must have a sister."

"No."

Later she recognized the undercurrent in that single syllable. In the moment, occupied with scrubbing, she said, "Really? It's only you and Cahill? And there's quite a gap in your ages, isn't there?"

"There is. We had a sister." Behind his matter-of-factness, something brought her gaze to his face. He kept plying the brush. "Closer in age to Cahill. I wasn't born when she died. Nor when our father died a few weeks later."

Her hands froze. "Oh, Kiernan."

"No sympathy for me," he instructed with would-be ease, still working. "As I said, I wasn't there to feel the loss. How can you miss what you've never had? All the sorrow and the loss fell to our mother and to Cahill. The sorrow most of all to Ma. For all she laughs and enjoys life now, there remains that sorrow, deep and wide. For the husband she loved so dear and for Patsy. Cahill, along with the sorrow and the loss, carried responsibility for so long. Not for our father, who was in an English hospital, hoping a specialist could work a miracle. But for Patsy. He was about young Dan's age when a confusion led to him and Patsy being put on a ferry back to Ireland without our mother. Cahill fought, trying to get himself and Patsy off and back to Mom. He was taken off all right, but Patsy went away on the ferry. There was a storm…"

"No." Dread smothered her.

"Patsy drowned, along with a number of others, but most were saved."

"Oh, Kiernan."

"No need for sorrow for me, Bexley. I never knew Patsy or our father. Mom was carrying me without knowing it, that's what made her sick, and started the confusion that led to Patsy being alone on the ferry."

"You can't possibly feel you were responsible—"

"Responsible? No. I didn't feel responsible."

Something was behind that, but before she could examine her certainty, much less ask anything, he went on.

"I knew naught of this for a long time. Not until I took Cahill's car and went off, intending never to return. It wasn't a well-thought-out plan—" His eyes gleamed with a hint of devilment. "—considering at that time I, too, was about young Dan's age and possessed a rudimentary understanding of driving a vehicle at best. But, ah, I was mad with anger at my brother."

"Why?"

"Responsibility. His motto, his strength, his burden. I see all that now. At that age I saw only that it was the word out of his mouth every other sentence and each of those sentences directed at me. When I ran away, Mom kept it from Cahill. He'd worked through the night with some emergency at the inn he owned by then and was sleeping in. Not that he'd have noticed his car gone six days out of seven as it was, because he worked every minute.

"Still, Mom shielded him from knowing what an ungrateful little— I'm sure you get the idea—I was. Mom searched for me herself and enlisted the help of a neighbor who was by way of being a distant cousin as well. I had the good fortune of fetching up against those folks first, rather than my mother. I don't suppose she would have spared me much at that moment. But nor would she have told me the history I needed to know. I have no doubt Mom and Cahill thought they were protecting me from hurt. But there came a time when the ignorance they left me in caused not only pain to me, but me causing them pain. My greatest regret."

"Did you… Did you tell them you knew? Did you talk about that history?"

"Not then. I hadn't given them cause to put any faith in me to that point, I needed to do that before we talked." A flicker of his grin flashed. "Or I was too scared. After Cahill came to America, Mom and I did talk. I needed her to know she could rely on me. As for Cahill, well, it was considerably easier to finally talk with him after he met and married Eleanor. He still has a way of treating me like more of a child than a man, teasing, especially about wom—" He stopped.

"Women? Is that what you were going to say?"

"It was. But as the words arose, I realized it was not entirely accurate, nor fair to my brother. He did, indeed, bedevil the life out of me over the girls I dated."

"Ah. The many, many girls you dated, from what I hear."

"The many girls I dated," he compromised.

"But not—" She paused, dropped her head to resume cleaning, but pushed through to the end. "—about the serious one?"

"No, not about her."

Despite keeping her head down, she knew he was looking at her.

"How much did Val tell you?" he asked.

"Not much. Pieces." She didn't mention other pieces came from other people.

Sometimes as if they forgot she hadn't known what happened with the woman Kiernan had thought was The One.

Sometimes as if they were willing her to know what was in their memories without saying the words straight out … but that was mostly Donna Currick.

"It's over and done with. Well in the past." Kiernan cleared his throat. "All in the past."

He closed the conversation, but couldn't stop her thoughts.

Over and done with. That's what she'd thought in July about Nigel.

Until she'd asked herself if she would have reacted so immediately to Kiernan's rejection if she'd been over it? Not over Nigel and the breakup—that truly was done with long before—but over the repercussions of the relationship.

Now… Yes, she thought she could claim that now. But could Kiernan?

She straightened her back.

"You're right." She was glad her voice came even, matter-of-fact.

"Am I? That's pleasant to hear. I'm not surprised, mind you. Though I've no idea what slice of my vast rightness you've spotted."

"We'll never get enough hubcaps clean to make a tree out of."

"I never said—"

She cut him off with a shake of her head. "You didn't need to. You're not that hard to read, you know." Her start on a smile ended abruptly, remembering how easy he'd been to read that night in July, especially at the end. She returned the conversation firmly to hubcaps. "At first I envisioned a triangle of shiny hubcaps from ceiling to floor as our two-dimensional tree. As we've worked on this one, I kept shrinking that vision and shrinking it, but now I have to admit that we couldn't even get six clean enough to do three—"

She drew her hand across the air.

"—two—"

A shorter air-drawn line above the first.

"—one."

A single dab at the top.

"You'll think of something else."

She renewed scrubbing, but with less vigor. They were close enough that they could at least finish this one.

Unexpectedly, he turned to her. "Why did you ask earlier if the story about your name bothered me?"

"Oh. Uh…"

"Your ex."

She exhaled. "Yeah. My ex didn't like my name. No. That's not right. He liked it fine until he knew how I got it. Then he was horrified. He'd thought it was a family name. Something polished with generations of poshness. A pair of poor grad students mistiming a trip to pick up a badly needed paycheck for manual labor didn't gibe with the image he wanted to project."

"Horrified, was he? Eejit."

"Eejit?"

"It's Irish for idiot.

"I like it." She grinned. The first time she had in association with a memory of Nigel. "And not to worry. The night he broke up with me—at his company party—I told as many of his bosses and colleagues the story as I could before I left—head held high."

"As it should be."

She felt her grin stiffen. "It was after that I fell apart. How could I be so wrong about someone?"

"People hide themselves. Some do. Those who want something."

Slowly, she nodded. "He wanted a woman with the right kind of name as part of the right image to reflect the right light on his image."

"Talk about an *amadán.*"

"A what?"

"It's an Irish word."

"It doesn't sound complimentary."

"It's not. Or he'd have wanted you, not a poor shadow he made up."

She skidded away from that. "My romantic history is no state secret, but how did you guess my ex had a role... Val?"

"No. She'd not trust me with your secrets. It was Matty. Not knowing she was spilling, I suspect."

"Doesn't matter. But why do you say Val wouldn't trust you with secrets."

He flicked her a look.

He'd noticed her changing the words from *her secrets* to the more general and oh, so much less personal *secrets.*

He rubbed hard, head down. "Val's known me a good, long while and with that comes my history of romances. Short stories for the most part."

"With you writing The End," she speculated.

Accurate speculation, he confirmed. "With me writing The End."

"Why?"

"Didn't find the right girl. Woman."

"But lots of wrong ones?"

"Not wrong ones. Nice ones. Lovely ones, but not the one for me."

"Why the grimace?"

She thought he wouldn't answer.

He thought he wouldn't answer—she could see that when he spoke, "Because when I thought I'd found the one for me, I couldn't have been more wrong."

CHAPTER TWENTY-SEVEN

"Felicity?"

So they had told her at least that much at the Slash-C. "Felicity's the name she told me. Changed the last name from the one Jack would have known."

When I asked who you are, I wasn't by way of asking your name. I put those pieces together. I was asking what kind of person would think to do such a thing as this…

"She came after me because of my connection to Jack. She used me to get to him. Nearly disrupted his and Val's wedding—no, *did* disrupt it, though she'd been going for destruction."

Every day. Every touch. Every moment together. Using him.

"Why? Why in the world would anyone try to hurt Jack and Val that way?"

He'd told Eric without much thought. Why not tell her?

But even as he used nearly the same straightforward words as he had with Eric, he kept hearing other words.

Words in the voice of the woman he'd thought he'd marry. Blaming Jack, despite the proof that another man had killed her sister and more young women.

It didn't change the years that had gone before. They were still there. … Knowing he got away with murder. And paid for nothing. For killing her. For ruining our family. For taking it all away. He did that. He did it all. … All except killing Hayley. The rest he did. We took him in to our family and loved him and he'd done that. So we closed off. No more taking anyone in. No loving anyone.

No loving anyone…

Was that what he was—?

"Have you seen her since then?"

Bexley's question broke him away from a dangerous thought.

"No." What he meant was no way in hell.

"Sounds like she really cared for you. Was—"

"*Cared* for me, is it? She—"

"—conflicted about what she did."

"—used me to try to get to Jack, to try to hurt people I care about. It was none of her doing that they were strong enough to get past it."

He kept scrubbing, but felt her watching him as she left an extra beat pass before saying, "Sounds like you're not over her. It's been—what?—a year and a half since Jack and Val's wedding. That's a long time. People can change. … Maybe you need to see her again, see if the two of you can get past what happened. Unless you're afraid—"

"Not afraid. Not interested. Wouldn't trust her to give me change for a penny."

"Trust is a choice. You decide to—"

"Is that what you did? A year-and-a-half for you, too, isn't it?"

A harsh reminder. But she responded calmly. "I didn't only trust him, I built my life, my business, my identity on who I was to him. Not on *me*, but what of me was reflected through him." She shook her head. "Can't believe I did that. Not doing it anymore. I know I'll be okay, no matter what. After this sum—"

She stopped abruptly.

After this summer…

They both knew it wasn't the season she meant. It was a night.

The end of a night.

She raised her chin. "But, yes, I have decided to trust. I've decided I have to. I can't go through life *not* trusting because someone pulled the rug out from under me."

As he had? That was how she saw that night, that was the movie in her head as Cahill said, that was why she ran? While he'd been so caught up in his own movie…

I know I'll be okay, no matter what.

Even a night that ended as theirs had.

He took after a spot and cleared it better than anywhere else.

After a couple more minutes, Bexley said, "Maybe…"

She stopped scrubbing, her eyes going unfocused and vague.

He waited to see if she'd add anything. Nope.

A smart man would let it lie.

He nudged, "Maybe, what?"

She didn't answer. Likely she didn't hear.

She dropped the cloth into the sink and walked out.

Kiernan looked at the cloth, turned to watch her departing back, then looked back to the wire brush in his hand, and the hubcap.

This close, might as well finish it.

He kept his focus on the hubcap, closing off all thoughts about his family, his past, his mistakes. Bexley.

Just focus on the hubcap. Transform it from filth to shine. This one hubcap. Couldn't do all of them for her—for them. The kids. Not enough time.

Time...

The timing was off for him and Bexley. Way off.

If they'd met before he'd fallen for a woman who—far worse than betraying him—had used him to hurt others, would he and Bexley...?

Maybe...

He scrubbed harder.

Maybe not.

Before Felicity, he'd sidestepped attachments. Mostly he'd dated women with sharp edges. That avoided many temptations. The others... He'd cut off the dating soon.

Would he have appreciated Bexley's warmth then? Or...?

He put enough muscle into the scrubbing that he loosened a patch he'd previously given up on.

Before his thoughts could take him down that path again, she came into the bathroom with the glow of a goddess carrying the standard of victory. Except what she held aloft was a can. Like bug aerosol cleaner or—

"The spray paint," she exulted. "Green spray paint. We'll spray paint a tree of hubcaps. And if some of the grime shows through, it will look like branches."

Gramps moaned, he griped, he declared they were defacing his property.

But he didn't come right out and say they couldn't spray paint a triangle of hubcaps green to resemble a Christmas tree. And he had plenty of opportunity to do that.

Because, first, they let the fire die down some and decided on an area away from the stove to create the tree, which meant moving hubcaps so the tree wouldn't be missing a chunk out of its far side. Then they broke down two thick boxes and folded them flat to slide into the diagonal gaps between hubcaps to keep the paint where they wanted it and away from where they didn't.

Bexley insisted on doing the painting. Eric would wield the box on the left side, with Pauline as backup if he needed, and Kiernan was on the right side with Dan as backup.

The three girls and Bobby were sent into the shop. Just in case.

"Supposed to do this in a ventilated space," Gramps grumbled, showing no sign of leaving his chair, though he'd been invited—several times—to join his younger grandchildren.

Dan laughed, startling the rest of them into swiveling their heads toward him. "If this place were any more ventilated, it'd be outdoors."

The rest of them chuckled. Gramps humphed.

Bexley drew in a deep breath.

"Okay, here we go."

Green paint on the cardboard proved the wisdom of using it. A slice of green on Kiernan's arm did little harm, since he and Eric had taken off their shirts to reveal short-sleeved t-shirts, and it would come off his skin.

The question of whether Kiernan in a t-shirt contributed to the mishap, Bexley eventually pushed to the back of her mind.

Bexley's fingers were well greened. She expected that would come off eventually, too.

But she regarded the finished product without joy. A fact she feared was clear to all of them.

"Good job," Eric said. "The perfect shape for a Christmas tree."

"You did an excellent job," Pauline said.

Dan ducked his head. "Looks good."

"Can we come in now?" Molly asked from the doorway between the store and the bar room.

"Come ahead. But don't touch it. It's still wet."

"It smells in here."

Lizzie stopped halfway across the room. "It's a tree. We have a Christmas tree."

"T'ee?" Bobby repeated, looking around.

"What's bothering you, Bexley?" Kiernan asked.

Before she could answer, Gramps from his chair called, "That's as bad as I thought it'd be. Can't hardly see it from here."

Hands on hips, she said, "*That's* what's bothering me. It's barely visible unless you're right on top of it."

Kiernan didn't dispute that.

Had she hoped he would? Her spirits dipped lower.

Kiernan, though, still stared at the wall. Then he gave a quick nod. He strode back to the wall, reached out, and took down one of the non-painted hubcaps next to the right edge of the "tree."

"Yeah." Eric began removing unpainted hubcaps from the left side of the tree.

With Dan assisting, they took down all the unpainted hubcaps, starting to stack them by the bar.

"Wait," Bexley said. "Let's put them by the stools. They'll make a lot of noise if Bobby gets too close to it."

"That helps. That definitely helps. Thank you all."

Was she thinking more of the Bobby barricade than the tree?

The wall was still dark with spots of less dark where the hubcaps had been, but even that amount of difference in color, aided by the difference in texture created more contrast.

"And the garlands," Bexley said.

The girls ran to the boxes behind the bar and carried the garlands to her in triumph.

The rest of them watched her zig-zag the garlands atop the tree, twisting, bending, fluffing them back to life.

She stepped back and looked at it critically.

"Wait," Kiernan said, "not done yet."

He went into the women's room and returned with the one cleaned hubcap. He took down the top green-painted hubcap of the "tree" and replaced it with the almost-shiny clean one.

"Oh," came from Lizzie, possibly Molly, too.

"Adds shine," Eric said.

Kiernan looked at Bexley.

She smiled.

"That's great. But it still needs one more thing."

He groaned humorously. "Of course it does."

CHAPTER TWENTY-EIGHT

She was right—naturally.

While everyone watched, she took red ribbon from two boxes of candy that must have been in the store cooler for a decade, waiting for some customer to desperately need apology candy. It would require desperation to buy this candy.

Bexley connected, then wound the ribbons through the pattern of openings near the hubcap rim and added an impressive bow.

"It should be a star at the top of a tree, but a wreath as a tree-topper suits our tree."

She handed it to Kiernan to put up. For a moment, their fingers and their gazes snagged.

She stepped back.

For another beat he remained still and solitary.

A quick breath, then he turned and placed the embellished hubcap at the top of the tree.

"Perfect," Pauline proclaimed.

Bexley clearly didn't think the tree rose to the level of perfect, but she nodded, declaring it done. Did she not realize she'd made something of nothing?

"Okay, let's get busy decorating our tree!"

They ate a simple dinner of soup, cheese, crackers, olives, and pickles. The chocolate chip cookies provided the highlight, supplemented with pudding cups, so they wouldn't eat all the cookies before Christmas Day.

As they hung the shiny stars—the shiniest being the handful Dan and his sisters collaborated on with thin cardboard covered in aluminum foil—on the tree by wires hooked into various hubcaps, the lights flickered.

Reminded of the storm, everyone stopped, looking up at the wagon wheel light.

"Did your family have a traditional Christmas Eve dinner when your daughters were growing up?" Pauline asked Gramps in a clear attempt to redirect everyone's attention.

"Naw. Ate whatever."

Bexley resumed hanging stars and the others followed.

"We had pizza last year. That's our tradition."

Molly had lobbied for another pizza dinner tonight, but there wasn't enough for a full dinner for everyone. They'd have to save that for lunch the day after Christmas. Surely they wouldn't be here any longer than that—

"It's not a tradition when you do it once," Dan scoffed.

"Is so."

"Is not."

Paying no attention to her siblings, Lizzie asked, "What does your family eat on Christmas Eve, Kiernan?"

"Oyster stew, salad, and soda bread."

"What's oyster stew?" she asked.

Diverted from her dispute with Dan, Molly asked, "Bread made out of soda?"

"One at a time. Oyster stew's made from oysters, of course. With a white sauce. Not like your beef stew."

"But what are oysters?"

"Ah, you've not had oysters, land-locked as you are. Oysters come from the ocean in a shell. You must be adept with a knife to get them free from that shell, eating them as fresh as possible. Their taste depends greatly on where they come from and the type. It's a lifetime's endeavor to sample all the kinds of oysters there are."

"Is that what you ate when you were our age in Ireland?" Lizzie asked.

"Ah, no. That's come from my American family. When I was your age, we had a white fish stew. In the old days—long, long before I was born, I'll have you know before you youngsters start calling me old enough to remember this, they had only potatoes in milk, butter, seasonings. Many didn't have more than that and what they did have they saved up for Christmas dinner and—of course—the Christmas cake."

"Christmas cake?" Lizzie repeated.

"How do you make that?" Molly added.

Bexley stirred uneasily at the signs of the girls' baking fervor snagging on that menu item.

"You start months and months before, making the cake, then wrap it up, taking it out regularly to feed it more whiskey or brandy."

"*Eww.*" Their noses wrinkled.

Gramps looked intrigued.

"Not for the youngsters," Kiernan agreed. "As well as not something to whip up in a minute. Because after all the feeding of whiskey and brandy, there's another icing goes all around, and that must harden for a time, too."

"Perhaps we can make another batch of chocolate chip cookies tomorrow for dessert," Pauline said. "But no Christmas cake."

The girls—and Dan—smiled at the prospect of the cookies.

But Molly wasn't done with questions. "What about the bread made from soda?"

"Not soda like you drink, but baking soda, like in the cookies," Bexley explained.

"That's right. Irish soda bread, now that's something I've eaten in Ireland and in Gloucester. It's traveled the world with me, you could say."

"Did our grandma eat that kind of bread?" Molly asked Gramps.

"Her? I don't know. Probably not unless she could get somebody else to pay for it."

Bexley jumped in. "Are you asking about your great-great-grandmother who came from Ireland?"

"Yeah, that one."

Gramps said, "Oh. Suppose so, if that's what they eat there."

Keeping the topic going, Bexley asked, "Did you eat special things for Christmas, Eric?"

"My family would always go to Andersonville in Chicago and bring home enough goodies to last through the winter."

"Andersonville? That's the Swedish neighborhood, right? The bakeries. Oh, the bakeries," Bexley said.

"You've obviously been," Pauline said dryly.

Eric grinned. "Mom's side of the family's Swedish. It was a required trip."

"What's your Christmas Eve tradition, Pauline?" Bexley asked.

"We opened presents. Then we all went to church at midnight."

Kiernan chuckled. "We went to church at midnight, too, then came home and kept wrapping, because we'd not one of us finished ahead of time. Nearly caught by Santa a time or two."

The girls' eyes widened.

"Santa," Bobby repeated wisely.

"And you, Bexley?"

"We'd clean up from dinner, then take a platter of all the kinds of Christmas cookies and sit around the tree, with a fire in the fireplace. At some point, Mom would go to the piano and we'd all sing Christmas carols." She swallowed, missing her family, missing that time. "And, of course, we hung our stockings and went to bed early so we didn't risk getting caught by Santa, which is what you all should be doing."

"I'm not tired." Molly yawned on the last word, without showing any sign of thinking that weakened her position.

Lizzie had a different objection. "But there isn't a fireplace here. And if we hang anything on the stove, it'll melt."

Everyone looked at Bexley.

She smiled at the girl. "No fireplace, but we have the absolutely perfect tree for hanging Christmas stockings."

And so, the four Quick children hung their makeshift Christmas stockings by hooking them on hubcaps.

The girls went first. Dan lifted Bobby to place his stocking at the same height, then put his own up—with minimal complaint or eye-rolling.

These four kids, standing hopefully in front of a triangle of hubcaps, for heaven's sake. Without their mother ever again, without their father for now—Bexley sent up another good thought for that worried and wearied man—with stockings stapled together, and presents improvised at best.

Yet their eyes sparkled—even Dan's a little—their mouths smiled. And they stood together. Close.

CHAPTER TWENTY-NINE

"They're tucked in," Pauline reported as she returned to the bar room from settling the girls and Bobby, "but as for asleep… I wouldn't be at all surprised if they come popping out at any moment. I'm going to wait to get back to those octopi. And this."

She placed a necklace of colored beads in front of Bexley on the table.

They all, Kiernan thought, looked to Bexley for direction.

"In the meantime, we can decide what we're going to do for Christmas dinner," she said.

"Feed them heartily at breakfast and maybe they won't notice," Pauline suggested. "We have plenty of eggs for a couple more breakfasts, even going extra tomorrow morning."

Gramps groaned. "Eggs're what folks come in here for first. That and milk and you're clearing me out."

"Nonsense. We're using things up before their expiration dates. By the time everyone digs out and gets moving again, you couldn't have sold these anyway."

"You'd be surprised," he mumbled, leaving it unclear whether she'd be surprised by how quickly after a blizzard Wyomingites were out buying eggs and milk or by their willingness to buy items past their expiration dates.

Bexley returned to the main issue. "Eggs are good, but we should do something special for Christmas breakfast—especially considering Christmas dinner won't include turkey and all the trimmings or—" She tipped her head toward Kiernan. "—goose or ham or—That's it!"

"There's no baked ham," Kiernan said. "I checked."

"No, but Gramps said there are ham sandwiches. The bread's

surely stale by now, but we can raid them for the ham and cook it up with the eggs. Separately or scrambled or omelets.”

“Good idea.”

Pauline’s approval came as Kiernan pushed back his chair, with Eric doing the same, their intentions clear.

“Hey. I can sell those sandwiches. They’re still good. Leave those sandwiches alone.”

At that objection from Gramps, Dan got up and joined the cooler-raiding party.

When they returned with two shopping bags full, Gramps groaned.

“This bread’s probably stale, too, but can you do anything with roast beef sandwiches?” Eric asked. “They hit their expiration date today, so did the ham. Tacos tomorrow. Dan spotted that.”

Obeying Bexley’s “Let’s see what we’ve got before we start tearing them apart,” they emptied the contents of the bags on the table.

Eric reached for one of the plastic-covered sandwiches to open the package.

“Wait,” Kiernan said. “Bexley’s got an idea.”

He could practically see her mentally disassembling the sandwiches into their component parts, then reassembling them into something else.

Without taking her eyes from the table, she asked, “What are the tacos made with?”

“Ground beef,” Dan said.

She smiled. Slow and wide.

“Got it. Dan, can you go back and gather up as many packets of catsup as you can find? And don’t worry, Gramps, none of this will go to waste. But it will take some work.”

Ham went in one dish, roast beef in another, ground beef in a third. The pieces of bread with mustard on them went in one pile, those without in another, the best slices of the “withouts” had their own pile. Cheese, lettuce, and tomato slices from the sandwiches had smaller plates. The shredded lettuce and cheese, along with beans from the tacos were lumped together.

"Are you going to tell us what this is all going to make?" Eric asked.

Kiernan found he didn't care what it would make. He enjoyed watching Bexley create.

"Christmas breakfast, Christmas dinner, and the day-after-Christmas breakfast."

"From *this*?" Eric smiled, but he doubted.

Kiernan didn't. She'd make magic of these deconstructed sandwiches and tacos.

"Along with a few other ingredients, led by eggs." She twirled one hand over the pile of the best slices of bread like a magician with a wand. "French toast for tomorrow morning." Next, she indicated the with-ketchup pile of bread and the ground beef. "The start of our Christmas dinner main course of meatloaf, with a seasonal red glaze starting from catsup." Another wave caught the lettuce and tomato. "Along with a salad." One more magic-wand hand wave encompassed the roast beef, the short middle stack of bread, and the taco fixings. "And a Tex-Mex stir-up for a hearty breakfast the day after Christmas."

Amid words of praise, Pauline beamed. Eric whistled. Even Gramps looked impressed. As for Dan ... he looked hungry, but that was how he always looked.

Belatedly, Kiernan realized that watching their reactions and—mostly—watching her, he hadn't contributed to the praise.

"We need more for dinner, though," she said. "Sides for the meatloaf."

"I saw spinach in the freezer," he said. Better than praise, he'd contributed something of use.

"Wonderful. Spinach will add more green to the table, along with the red catsup glaze. And if we put enough butter on those dried potatoes in the boxes—"

"Will you and the other kids eat spinach?" Eric asked Dan.

"No way."

Bexley deflated.

Kiernan wanted to have a few words with the kid.

Before that could happen, though, Pauline spoke. "My mother used to mix chopped spinach into any number of dishes when we were children. I never knew that until I was an adult and complained that the recipes she'd shared with me did not taste the same as my childhood memories."

Bexley's smile re-ignited. Kiernan would vote for chopped spinach in every dish imaginable if it always produced that smile.

"The kids might eat it that way," Dan allowed, hinting that he—knowing what was in the meatloaf—might not. Kiernan bet the boy's teenage appetite would overcome an aversion to spinach once it was hidden in ground beef.

"Great. My mother also puts bacon in meatloaf, so we can use that package that was too small for everybody to have some at breakfast. Okay, let's get busy with this. Who'll chop spinach?"

"I will," Kiernan said quickly, before anyone else jumped on that opportunity to help her.

She accepted with a smile. "Eric and Dan, will you tear up this stack of bread with the mustard on it for the meatloaf? Small pieces. And Pauline, if you'll wrap the makings for the two breakfasts?" Clearly, that was the most technical job. "We'll have to be very quiet going through the bedroom to the kitchen so we don't wake the kids."

The good news from Kiernan's point of view was his task put him in the kitchen with Bexley, beginning the meatloaf, after she stopped in the store for the bacon and a few other ingredients.

Even though she and Pauline spent most of the time discussing meatloaf.

To the ground beef she'd put in the pot standing in for a mixing bowl, Bexley added French onion dip.

"Always used instant soup myself," Pauline said. "But this should work, especially if you use less milk."

Bexley nodded, opening and adding other packets. "No Worcestershire sauce, but the soy sauce should give it some zing. Now for the catsup."

"How'd you learn to cook?" Kiernan asked Bexley.

He caught Pauline looking between them.

"From my Mom. Dad, too. Once we reached high school, we each shared in the cooking. Practical people, my parents. We also had lessons in laundry, bed-making, cleaning, car maintenance, and finances."

"That's why you do videos on those topics."

Bexley cut him a look without letting their gazes meet. "Yes, the ones I'm doing now."

The ones she knew he must have watched since the summer because she hadn't started them until after… After.

"You did a different kind of video before?" Pauline didn't look up from her ministrations with plastic wrap and aluminum foil.

This time, Bexley's and Kiernan's gazes met. Hers bounced away.

He'd introduced the topic of her videos, but left plenty of buffer space for her to avoid mentioning her previous work.

"Yes. Lifestyle videos—a different kind of lifestyle, when I was living a different life. Since—the past several months, I switched to practical ones. It's amazing how many people don't know the things our parents taught us. Are you finished with the spinach?" she asked him while focusing on adding salt and pepper to the mix in the big pot.

"I'm not at all surprised," Pauline said. "Although you've gone beyond the practical here—"

"Creative." Kiernan stepped in close to her—there was no choice in this tiny kitchen. "All done chopping."

"Precisely. Creative. Is—?"

Bexley interrupted Pauline. "Ah, Eric," she greeted him with pleasure. A bit of relief, too?

She also tried to move away from Kiernan, but Eric's arrival cut off her retreat.

"Breadcrumbs," Eric announced.

"Perfect timing. Put them right in here."

"Chopped spinach in there, too?"

"Yes, thank you." She backed up and sidestepped to the sink, avoiding contact with Kiernan. "Will one of you do the bacon? Gramps' lack of kitchen utensils means I'll mix this with my hands.

Hated that as a kid—*eww, gross*—though I've come to appreciate it. It's the best way to ensure you don't overmix it, which can make your meatloaf tough."

She hadn't been nervous until he'd moved in close. Yet she seemed fine being around Eric.

Kiernan, maintaining possession of the knife when Eric would have volunteered, had the bacon diced in record time. After he added that to the pot, he leaned back against the counter and watched from half-lowered eyelids.

"Isn't meatloaf supposed to be a loaf?" Eric looked down into the pot.

Bexley chuckled. "It is, but no loaf pan, no baking dish and no way our improvised cookie sheets couldn't hold this. At least the frying pans can go in the oven. Even this bigger one's not big enough to form a loaf from one side to the other, so I'm going to make it round."

"Sort of a theme with the hubcap Christmas tree."

She chuckled a lot longer than Eric's mild comment warranted.

With the meatloaf carefully molded into a ring in the frying pan, Pauline even more carefully wrapped it with plastic, then aluminum foil.

"Okay, that's done," Bexley said with satisfaction, closing the refrigerator once it was stored.

"Now we have to finish the octopi, divide the necklace, and stuff the stockings," Pauline said.

It was going to be a late night.

CHAPTER THIRTY

Gramps disappeared, but they were all so busy, his absence was barely noticed.

Kiernan and Eric volunteered to scour the store for stocking stuffers.

Pauline divided the necklace with Dan as an assistant, adding thread from her sewing kit to make sure the new necklaces would fit over the girls' heads.

Bexley commandeered three white socks from Kiernan—when he joked about what use the fourth sock might be, she took that, too.

She cut off the toes, tied off the opening with Pauline's thread, poured rice from the store into it, tied off the top to hold it in, then cinched the middle to form a two-ball snowman. Turning back the edge of the toe, she formed a hat for each. Then Pauline sewed on buttons—saved from Gramps' sacrificed shirts—for eyes and a mouth.

Bexley found more ribbons from a beer display old enough to have faded in places. By careful placement, she hid the faded spots as she tied a jaunty scarf on each sock snowman.

She placed each in a red plastic bag, tying Gramps' twine into a bow to close it, and fluffing out the tops.

"That's fantastic, Bexley," Pauline said. "Afraid the octopi won't fit in those bags, though. Any ideas what to do with them?"

"I thought we'd use the six-pack bottle holders. We'll need to cut out the interior dividers, then cover them with the old Christmas cards."

"You are amazing." The older woman's admiration quickly turned to brisk orders. "Eric, Kiernan, get those holders and start taking out the interiors."

Stuffing the stockings was a delicate matter, with one person holding and another carefully placing in the items.

Pens and pencils, erasers in the shape of animal faces, toothpaste, toothbrushes, lip protector for the cold, combs, a pack of playing cards for each. They even wrapped the card packs inside the Christmas cards' decorated envelopes from the attic boxes.

A refrigerator magnet for each, with a note attached that it was to hang an important item on their fridge at home.

Pauline and Bexley raided their toiletries kits for travel-sized body lotion and moisturizer for the girls.

In the back-to-school pack Dan spotted, they found washable markers for Bobby, colored pens divided between the girls and held together with stretchy glittery bands meant for other merchandise, notebooks for each, a calculator for Dan that he acknowledged with wry recognition of where it came from as he watched it go in.

A small bag of candy each.

They pooled their change to drop some in each stocking, then added a few dollar bills to each.

Bexley was sure she'd seen Kiernan add a five to Dan's stocking when no one else was looking.

The boy missed it because he'd stretched out on his bed on the floor and promptly fell asleep.

"Now to finish the octopi." Pauline spread a blanket over Dan on her way back to the table where those fabric creations awaited.

She padded the balls they were using for heads with the pieces of discarded fabric from Gramps' shirts. They draped the fabric strips over the balls, tying off the short ends for a "hair" tuft, then under the ball, leaving lengths of fabric streaming down.

Then she and Bexley braided—and braided and braided—to create eight fabric legs for each octopus, while Kiernan and Eric applied Christmas cards to the modified six-pack carriers, with frequent consultations with the two women.

Gramps reappeared with three simple wood dinosaurs, now sanded smooth. He put one in each of his younger grandchildren's stockings, then grumbled about it being past midnight and lowered himself into his own bedroll by the stove.

One octopus leg short of being done, they ran out of thread or ribbon to tie it off.

Eric went to search the store once more for something appropriate. Impatient he hadn't returned yet, Pauline followed.

"Meant to tell you, I checked the cord on the little ceramic tree. It's fine to plug in," Kiernan said.

Bexley meant to thank him, but yawned so widely she lost control of the braid-in-progress in her hand.

Kiernan half rose to lean across the corner of the table and plant one finger at the last firm point of the braid, pinning it to the table, so she didn't lose more of her work.

"Go to bed, Bexley. You're beat."

"Everybody's been up as long as I have."

"Nobody's worked harder or made up more stuff. That takes energy. Get some rest. You have more to do tomorrow."

"I'll finish this and—"

"I'll finish it."

She looked up in surprise at the intensity in his voice and encountered a bigger surprise.

Kiernan had leaned close, his head just above hers. She looked up directly into his eyes, his mouth a small downward swoop from hers. … Or a small upward swoop if she weren't so incredibly tired. And if she didn't feel another yawn rising around her throat, controlling her jaw muscles, bending her mouth to its will. Just in time, she slid her hand over her mouth as it gaped open again.

As soon as it was past, she said the first thing that occurred to her. "You can braid? That last part needs to be rebraided."

"Cahill taught me. Twisted rope—well, it twists. We mostly bought rope for sailing and such, but Cahill insisted I know how to make it, too. Now, go on with you. You've worked yourself too hard. Go to bed, Bexley."

And the raspy way he said it had her thinking the words could so easily have been *Come to bed, Bexley. Come to bed with me. Now.*

Oh, yeah, she was beyond tired if she was thinking that.

"I just want to make it fun for those kids. Losing their mother…" She stopped to swallow down abrupt tears. "Those poor kids."

"And their father. My mother's heartbreak penetrated even my child's brain … eventually. When—"

He broke off, as if belatedly realizing he'd spoken the words aloud.

He glanced toward her. She'd been looking at him, but ducked her head before their eyes met. "Yes," she said softly, "and their father."

"Better not to open to such sorrow." When she didn't respond to his harsh words, he added the challenge, "Isn't it?"

"Closing off any possibility of sorrow would mean having no love at all. Would you give up the love of your nephew, of all the next generation of the Slash-C crew in case something ever happened to them?"

She looked up at him now and saw two things.

He'd recognized her shift from discussing one kind of love to another.

His inability to imagine not loving the kids she'd seen him with at the ranch.

"I'll die before them. I'm that much older."

"If everything follows a neat pattern. But life doesn't always, does it?" Not awaiting an answer, she jerked back her chair. "I will take you up on your offer to finish up. Thank you. Good night."

At the doorway, she turned back and softly said, "Merry Christmas, Kiernan."

CHAPTER THIRTY-ONE

Three months and six days ago

Kiernan's finger lingered over the button on the computer that would open Bexley Farber's new website. The portal to her new venture. To the photos. The videos.

He'd known when it went live more than a month ago. He hadn't looked at any of it.

But, surely, that was being overly cautious. It wasn't like the flesh and blood woman would appear in front of him. There could be no repeat of… No repeat.

It was natural to be curious about what she'd made of the plans she'd been working on.

The movie in her head that Cahill had hypothesized? No, that he'd never know.

But this? This was simply curiosity.

He clicked the button.

"Hi. I'm Bexley Farber."

Bexley smiled at him from the screen. Into him.

CHAPTER THIRTY-TWO

December 25

Bexley heard the girls and Bobby stirring.

Why did Christmas morning always come so fast for adults and so slow for children?

She'd been exhausted when she fell into bed. But she could almost swear she'd heard sounds from the bar room, like the guys were moving furniture. That lasted a few seconds until she'd fallen asleep.

Which seemed about sixteen seconds ago.

Though when she opened one eye a slit, the room had a faint lessening of the darkness, despite the storm still reigning outside.

Her phone made a low sound. A text. Her family, hoping to get through with a Christmas wish? With her back to the girls, she surreptitiously slid the phone off the bedside table and under the sheet she had pulled up high. If they didn't know she was awake, maybe they'd give her a few more minutes of rest.

The text was from Kiernan. *Give us as much time as you can. Will text when ready.*

From the wide recliner, childish whispering resolved into snatches of words revolving around wondering if the adults were awake yet.

Bobby took care of that issue by sliding out of the chair, padding across to Pauline on the near side of the bed and thunking her on the shoulder. "Wake now? Wake? Wake?"

She groaned. Bexley might have, too.

But she sat up in bed, which brought Bobby running around to her side, joyously yelping, "Wake! Wake! Wake!"

"Yes, I am awake." She slid her phone toward Pauline, tapping the screen to bring her attention to the text.

Molly exulted, "Yay! We can go out and see if Santa—"

"No," she said quickly to the girls. "We're all going to look nice for Christmas before any of us leave the room."

Groans.

Pauline cut them short. "Of course we all want to look nice for Christmas Day. First, you girls decide what you're going to wear while I get ready in the bathroom and clean up Bobby."

Relegated to one of the "girls," Bexley put on her robe, feeling gratitude to skip Bobby cleanup duty.

Until the debate began on what Molly and Lizzie were going to wear.

Both wanted to wear the same star-studded pair of leggings that were in Lizzie's bag but Molly insisted were hers. Neither wanted to wear any of the tops in either bag. Both lamented they didn't have with them what they *really* wanted to wear, which included three tutus, a robe, a cape, two crowns, a parasol, and a favorite pair of plaid shorts.

To distract them—or perhaps herself—Bexley took out her planned outfit for the day. A shimmery red tunic over a black tank and a pair of flowy pants. She looked at them lying on the bed and reconsidered. They'd do great for her parents' home, but perhaps weren't the best choice for this place and time.

"That's beautiful." Lizzie's gaze lasered on the shimmery tunic.

Molly dismissed the solid colors. "Kind of boring."

"What's that?" Lizzie pointed to something in a similar tone to the tunic.

"That's—" Bexley broke off from explaining it was a simple t-shirt. "Would you like to wear it, Lizzie? With your black leggings and your red boots—"

"I'd look like you," the little girl said in awe. "Oh, yes, please."

Bexley hugged her. "Some of the time I'll be dressed as well as you are. Not all the time. I was thinking with the cooking I need to do, I might wear a sweatshirt and jeans part of the time." She refolded the flowy pants and tucked them back into her bag. "These will wait for another time."

She drew out the t-shirt, which would fit Lizzie fine as a dress.

"I can wear jeans and a sweatshirt," Molly said.

Lizzie offered, "You can wear the star pants." Unspoken but still communicated was the added, *Since I'm wearing a special outfit.*

"You know what would go great with the star pants? This black t-shirt with a scarf we could use as a belt."

She'd barely begun the hunt for the scarf she had in mind when Pauline came out with a still-damp Bobby.

Bexley shepherded the girls into the bathroom to oversee them as they washed their faces and brushed their teeth, even slipping in those ablutions for herself.

Then she captivated the girls' attention by putting on mascara and what amounted to lip gloss. You'd think from their reactions she was putting on the glam for the Oscars.

When they came out, Pauline was dressed in a dark green top with a Christmas broach on the lapel over black slacks. Bobby had on a clean shirt and pants. No one expected that to last, but he'd start the day in high fashion.

A knock on the bedroom door lifted Bexley's hopes that Kiernan had opted for that signal rather than texting. But it was Gramps, calling out his demand that he be allowed use of his own bathroom.

They let him in. He gathered a few clothing essentials from the dresser and closet, then repaired to the bathroom, the clicking sound leaving no doubt he'd locked the door.

The girls dressed—all too quickly for Bexley's taste, because a peek at the phone showed no follow-up message from Kiernan.

Bexley stood them side by side. "Let me look at you two… Hmm. You both look good, but could you look better?"

"No," Lizzie said.

"Yes," Molly said. "It's boring."

"Okay, let's re-think this." She crossed her arms and considered them, as if they were sculptures in an art museum. Though few art museums made art lovers squeeze past the corner of a bed or dodge sideways to avoid a staggering toddler.

Lizzie giggled.

Molly remained solemn, clearly counting on Bexley to fix *boring.*

"You need more pattern, Molly. Something Christmassy." She went to her bag. She blocked their view with her body, despite Molly craning her neck, then spun around with her family tradition pajama top. "How about this as a jacket."

"*Yes.*"

Good thing she hadn't followed the family tradition last night. The PJs were pristine.

Satisfaction didn't last long.

"That jacket will look better with the black leggings and—"

"I get the star pants," Lizzie exulted. "They'll look good with this *solid* color."

"They looked good with *this*. Two patterns are better than one." Did Molly get that gene from her grandfather? "Look. There're are stars in the jacket, too."

They glared at each other. This did not bode well for their teen years.

"It's Christmas," Pauline quietly reminded them.

Bexley swooped into their temporarily chastised state. "Let's do this—star pants to Lizzie. Christmas jacket to Molly. And each of you has a scarf for a belt."

After a moment's hesitation, Molly said, "I get to pick the scarf."

She drove a hard bargain, especially when she determined none of Bexley's were "interesting" enough. Pauline finally pleased her with a shimmery silver scarf. "New Year's Eve," she said to Bexley.

"It might get creased or—"

"It's fine."

She put it on Molly herself. They smiled at each other.

"Ready." Molly headed for the door.

"Wait." Bexley looked to Pauline for inspiration, but received a shrug. Bexley put her hand to her head, wishing she could drag an idea out of it. "*Hair!* We have to fix our hair."

First, she brushed each girl's hair with deliberate absorption. She tried the same with Bobby, but he wiggled away across the bed.

She combed her own hair, then twisted it up. Decided the first and second time wouldn't do, and took a third try.

"Can we wear our hair like yours?" Lizzie asked.

With that promise of using up more time, Bexley decided her most recent version of her hairdo was fine.

"Of course."

She added commentary as she put up each girl's hair, telling them they could do this for each other.

And then they were done.

She had to think of something else. "Molly, I think I should re-do yours. It might fall—"

The faint trill of her phone receiving a text sent her diving for it.

Ready.

Watching her face, Pauline said, "I think Molly's hair looks perfect. Does it feel secure?"

"Sure." The girl nodded vigorously. "See?"

"I guess it does look secure." Bexley confirmed Pauline's speculation that the text released them from their stalling duty with a slight nod.

Pauline rapped on the bathroom door. "Are you done primping in there?"

In retrospect, Bexley recognized quite a bit of time had elapsed since the shower had turned off.

"Hold your horses, woman!"

Unfazed, Pauline informed him through the door. "You'd best hurry up. We're all going out now to greet Christmas."

Kiernan, Eric, and Dan were in a clump by the doorway to the bar room, covered by the closed curtain panels. Along with a haze of dust that Bexley would bet came from the curtains.

"Merry Christmas!" the girls trilled in harmony. Bobby added a "Mare Chri'ma" counterpoint.

"Merry Christmas to you. Wait—" Kiernan stopped them when they would have pushed aside the curtain and gone into the bar area. "We need to tell you. Something happened during the night."

"What? What happened?" Molly hopped from one foot to the

other, while Lizzie kept Bobby from falling over when he tried to emulate her.

"We woke up and—No, we need to wait for everybody and we'll all go in together. All I can say is whoever did this must have been fast and very quiet, because it didn't wake any of us up. Unless… Did you wake up and see anything, Dan?"

"Nope. Not a thing."

"He can sleep through anything," Molly scoffed.

"Daddy says it's like trying to pry up a rusted nail without a hammer to get him out of bed," Lizzie added.

"Didn't wake me up, either." Eric's declaration redirected the girls' attention to the covered door.

"But what is it? What happened in there?" Molly asked.

"What? What?" Bobby echoed.

They looked from Eric to Kiernan, even to Dan, then back.

Those three all shook their heads.

Bexley hoped they weren't building it up so much that the kids would be disappointed.

"You'll have to wait until your grandfather joins us," Pauline declared.

The girls sent their visual appeal first to Bexley, who shrugged, then to Kiernan, who crossed his arms over his chest, enhancing his bouncer-guarding-the-door pose.

"But he's taking for*ever*," complained Molly.

Dan made a sound that had them all turning toward him, then redirecting their attention to where he was looking, the door to the bedroom.

All the females and Bobby turned around to see what was behind them.

"Gramps," the girls said together, then appeared to have nothing to add to that.

Bobby came to the rescue of all his tongue-tied elders.

"*Santa.*"

CHAPTER THIRTY-THREE

Santa applied to Gramps with only the loosest, most generous of interpretations.

On the other hand, it was that kind of Christmas.

So the portly figure with the white collar of a dress shirt showing above a bright red sweater molded to a bowl-full-of-jelly belly could stretch to stand in for the real thing.

Especially since he'd trimmed his beard to a neat oval that would do any Father—or Grandfather—Christmas proud. No more unshorn-hedge sides, no more straggly points, no more bushiness obscuring his mouth.

Nor did his hair stick out in odd directions. Both hair and beard were significantly whiter, a fact that Bexley pushed to the back of her mind with the determination to enjoy the improvement and not think about the baseline.

Bobby ran to Gramps, reaching up to take his hand, with no apparent concern that such a gesture might be spurned.

He was right.

The little boy then led his grandfather to the closed curtains.

" 'Prise," he informed his companion.

"May I?" Gramps asked of Kiernan, Eric, and Dan. They all nodded.

With his free hand, Gramps took hold of one side of the curtain and drew it back, as if he'd been a showman all his life.

"After you," he said with a slight bow to Pauline.

She took Eric's offered arm—keeping a straight face when he grinned at her—and advanced majestically into the darkened room.

The girls looked at Dan. "Go on. Go in," he said.

Each girl took one of his hands, whether from sibling fondness, a bit of nervousness over what came next, or a sense of the momentousness of the moment.

Dan cemented the momentousness by limiting himself to a single martyred sigh of the teenager indulging younger siblings as he escorted them over the threshold.

Gesturing Bexley to follow the others and keeping his eyes on her all the while, Kiernan slid his hand in along the wall and flipped the light switch.

Gasps—delighted and appreciative—came from Bobby and all the females.

In a spotlight that left the rest of the room in flattering softness, the hubcap tree stood noble and festive. The decorations glowed in the bright light, winking and sparkling with what looked like happiness.

"It's... It's *beautiful.*" Molly's words broke the frozen moment.

She, Lizzie, and Bobby surged forward.

Kiernan's hand at her back urged Bexley forward, too.

"What did you—? How did you...?" she asked in half questions.

He grinned at her, as delighted as the littles. "Had an idea. Eric and Dan and I pulled it off."

"I thought I heard—Were you moving furniture last night?"

"Moved the tables to get to the light. But took a fair amount of fine-tuning this morning."

Wresting her gaze from his face, she looked up. The wagon wheel light was tipped up on one side and tied in place to send all its illumination toward the tree, a spotlight picking up the glitter and shine of the top hubcap, each snowflake, star, and garland distributed over its surface.

"It's made all the difference," she said.

"If there weren't a tree there in the first place—which was all your inspiration—there'd be nothing to light up."

"Bexley, Bexley. Our stockings are *full* and there are *presents,*" Molly called out in awe.

"Santa really did come," Lizzie said. "I thought I heard him, but I couldn't be sure..." She moved forward in a seeming trance.

"Wonder if Santa spoke about meatloaf in her dreams?" Kiernan whispered into Bexley's ear.

She turned, smiling.

Close.

Too close.

But this time she didn't back away.

"Bexley, come see," Molly said.

She obeyed, yet held Kiernan's gaze an extra beat before turning to the children's joy.

Not only did the cheerful red bags and card-covered six-pack carriers under each of the three stockings look particularly festive in the kind light from the wagon wheel, but a small, white, awkwardly wrapped package had joined them under the girls' stockings, along with a similar one beneath Dan's, plus something wrapped in more of the old cards. A box, not wrapped, but with a squashed and dusty bow sat beneath Bobby's stocking.

Bexley, Kiernan, Pauline, and Eric exchanged looks that said none of them knew where those additions came from.

There was no time for more, because the girls were hopping from foot to foot in their eagerness to get to their stockings.

Bexley, Kiernan, and Eric took down the stockings with care, then settled on the bedrolls with the kids to hold onto the seams as they were explored. Gramps pulled up two chairs—side by side, Bexley noted—for himself and Pauline.

The girls and Bobby *ooh*ed and *aah*ed over each of the small, practical items in their stockings.

"Dine-s'r!" Bobby shouted when the wood form emerged. "Look, Dan, dine-s'r."

"Pretty cool, huh, squirt." Dan didn't even try to hide his grin.

"I have one, too," Lizzie exulted.

Molly reached deeper and found hers with a huge smile.

The playing cards also fascinated Bobby, who unwrapped the pack from the seasonal envelopes with meticulous attention … then played with the envelopes for several minutes.

"Oh, we'll have so many things to show the other kids when we get back to school," Lizzie said.

"Not the candy. I'm eating mine," Molly declared.

"Not now. Breakfast first," Bexley said. "Presents after breakfast. We need everybody to help. We need the table set, milk poured, coffee made, things brought out, and we'll start cooking."

Perhaps because of hunger pangs from the late start on breakfast, help came from everybody except Bobby, busy taking his cards out of the cardboard box, spreading them all over the floor, and sending some on apparent missions of great import with long explanations to his grandfather.

The French toast was an exorbitant hit with the four Quicks, who said they'd never had the treat before. The lack of maple syrup didn't bother them in the least, not with strawberry preserves and confectionary sugar atop the crispy, eggy bread slices.

Bexley and Pauline cooked up every piece of bread they'd set aside for French toast the night before, then another fresh loaf—Gramps didn't even complain, possibly because his mouth was full. In between, they ate the crisped and warmed ham. Kiernan and Eric shuttled back and forth from the kitchen to the bar room with the French toast, until they insisted Bexley and Pauline sit and enjoy the toast of their labor, too.

"That was delicious," Molly said.

The others mmm'd agreement.

"Presents now, right?"

"Presents," Bexley agreed. The dishes could wait.

Bobby unwrapped his octopus first and immediately found its shape perfect for being tucked against his heart with one chubby arm around its neck. Pauline's eyes misted, and even Gramps grinned—an expression visible now that he'd trimmed his beard.

The divided-in-two necklace from Pauline was a huge hit, each girl immediately adding it to her ensemble.

Each hugged her octopus and snowman with huge smiles.

Bobby pulled the bow off the otherwise plain box and put it on his head. With help from Lizzie, he took the top off the box to disclose twenty-six wooden blocks, each with a letter of the alphabet and illustrations of items starting with that letter.

They were in good shape, but old-fashioned.

More looks zipped around, centering on Gramps, but he focused on Bobby, extracting the "J" block from the box, while his sisters poured out explanations of letters, words, and reading.

"When he disappeared last night… Do you think…?" Bexley murmured to Kiernan.

"I do. Those boxes never went back in the attic. This should tell."

Kiernan nodded toward the two sisters, unwrapping their final presents.

Molly had hers open first. She turned it around in her hands. "It's like a barrette."

"It *is* a barrette, a beautiful pearl barrette," Pauline said.

"I have one, too," Lizzie said. "Bexley, will you put it in my hair."

"Of course, I will. There. The perfect addition."

After she performed the same service for Molly, Bexley looked around at Gramps.

"What?" Gramps demanded of her with a faint imitation of his usual irascibility.

Pauline tapped his arm. "You know *what*. You tell them, is there something special…?"

He cleared his throat twice, before saying, "You won't leave me in peace if I don't, will you, woman?" That clearly needed no response. He gusted a sigh. "Those barrettes… Your mama wore those barrettes the day she married your Daddy."

The girls' eyes widened.

"Mommy's?"

The soft, unified whisper felt like a fist to Bexley's heart.

Gramps cleared his throat yet again. "Those blocks were hers, too. Angie and Trudi's." He looked at his older grandson. "What about you, boy? You going to open those packages or hatch 'em?"

The first of the two presents under the hubcap tree for Dan turned out to be a shaving kit—Kiernan and Eric had pooled their resources and Pauline contributed a navy blue toiletries bag, transferring her things to a plastic bag.

Dan colored and said a gruff thanks that made him sound remarkably like his grandfather.

"I thought you said you knew nothing about those packages," Bexley whispered to Kiernan, because he was the closest of the three conspirators.

"Me? Didn't say a word." He did that *dinna* thing again with the word *didn't* and Bexley fought a shiver. "Besides, I meant this one he's opening now."

The second package looked like a hot dog wrapped in white paper with a scrap of ribbon tied inexpertly around its middle.

The teenager removed the ribbon as if he expected the package to blow up, then slowly unswaddled what was inside.

Aware of intensity behind her, Bexley turned and saw Gramps riveted on his grandson's motions.

She caught the others' eyes and shifted hers to Gramps, cluing in all of them to the mini-drama playing out.

With his head still down, Dan said, "It's… it's your whittling knife. The one your father…"

Dan looked around at his grandfather, his vulnerability pushing Bexley toward tears the boy would never forgive if he spotted them.

"I got another knife." Gramps made it a growl, failing to mask the clog in his throat. "You got a good start on your whittlin'. Time this went to another generation. You teach Bobby, when he's of an age."

"You'll teach him." Dan hesitated an added beat, then said, "Sir."

"What about us?" Molly demanded.

Dan reached over to rub the top of her head. She tilted away. "Not my hair! Bexley did my hair."

"He'll teach you all, squirts."

Taking that in the spirit it was meant but would never be acknowledged, Molly and Lizzie beamed at him.

CHAPTER THIRTY-FOUR

After the belated cleanup from breakfast, a lovely, satisfied lull settled over them all. Even the wind and snow seemed to take a break.

Dan and his grandfather started new whittling projects with Pauline watching complacently from a nearby chair. They spread a blanket in front of the stove and the rest of them sat there, playing with Bobby and the blocks until his yawning became contagious.

Bexley knew precisely when Kiernan leaned back against the wall and closed his eyes. She held a *shhh* finger to her lips.

The girls, aglow with the conspiracy of it, took Bobby for a cleanup and to take his nap.

Bexley and Eric chatted quietly about his law practice, her new online endeavor, their mutual friends in Wyoming, their Midwestern childhoods.

When the girls returned, they were chattering excitedly, but dropped their voices abruptly as they came in the room—too soon to catch what they were saying. They went immediately to Pauline, who might have been drifting off, judging by the way she jumped at their touch.

If so, she must have come fully awake when Molly and Lizzie pulled her from her chair and tugged her to the store.

Bexley and Eric exchanged looks—both asking the question, neither having the answer.

"What are they up to?" Eric wondered.

"What's going on, then?" Kiernan asked, stretching awake.

Bexley looked away from that sight, but said with passable equanimity, "The girls seem to be drawing Pauline into a conspiracy. I suppose it's a second batch of chocolate chip cookies."

They had no better idea when Pauline appeared at the entryway and announced, "None of you are to come in the kitchen—or the bedroom."

"It's my bedroom," Gramps automatically complained.

No one—least of all Pauline—appeared to consider that worth a response.

"I'll need to put the meatloaf in at five," Bexley said.

"If we're that long, I'm perfectly capable of putting it in the oven."

"The bathroom—"

Pauline cut off Kiernan's protest, delivered with mischief in his eyes. "You have the restrooms out here. No exceptions. Stay out."

Bexley raised her hands in a combo shrug and surrender. "Okay. I'll get the table ready then."

"Need help?"

Eric barely had the words out, before Kiernan said, "I'll help her."

"I don't think I'll need any help. Thanks, guys."

"Okay. Then I'm going to stretch out for a few minutes, maybe catch a nap."

"Good idea, Eric. You can get more of a nap, too, Kiernan."

"No need. What do you need done?"

"Um. Wipe the table, I guess. I'm going into the store, looking for ideas."

She spent far more time trolling the aisles of the store than she needed to.

Even after a second circuit of all the aisles to be sure she hadn't missed anything with potential, she hesitated to return to the warmth of the bar room.

It made no logical sense, but she was feeling even more jumpy and awkward around Kiernan now than at the beginning of this trip.

It *had* made sense at the start, considering … well, considering. No need to think about the details of that.

But they'd gotten past that. Working together, along with everybody else. All of them getting along like buddies.

Buddies…

His mouth close to hers. Their gazes holding.

His raspy voice telling her to go to bed, echoing with whispers of *Come to bed with me.*

Maybe not buddies.

But they could be. They *would* be.

If she could stay away from him for a while. Distance, that was what she needed. Distance and perspective.

Sure, there'd been looks, perhaps moments a wild optimist could interpret a certain way, but that wild optimist would get herself in trouble. Again. After all, the man's attitude about love bringing sorrow was as good as a proclamation that he had no interest in a relationship. And that was good. Really good. Because it gave her the fact she needed to make the wise decision of staying away from him.

If only she *could* stay away from him.

Instead of stuck in a blizzard in three rooms.

Three rooms?

Whatever the girls and Pauline were up to had them in two rooms. And the one of those she was in now was about to freeze her nose off.

She squared her shoulders.

She was going back in there and prepare the table for Christmas dinner for those kids. And she would be strictly buddies with Kiernan McCrea. She would.

She stepped back. "There."

"It looks great," Kiernan said.

"Great's too strong." She smiled without meeting his eyes.

She'd done that a lot while they—mostly she—set up the table.

She'd wrangled a sheet from Gramps to use as a tablecloth—not even stepping over Pauline's boundaries, since it was in a closet in the hallway between the shop and the bedroom. Atop the tablecloth, she fashioned a red runner from red tissue paper she'd found tucked away in the store.

He'd wondered about the purpose of the two white coffee cups from near the coffeemaker she'd brought in. She used them upside down and spread apart on the runner to each support a plate. Atop the raised plates, she'd created vignettes with a green-painted paper tree in the center of each, surrounded by candles from Gramps' boxes of decorations.

Then, with leftover strips of the tissue paper, she oh-so-carefully tied red bows around white napkins, turning utilitarian into festive at each place around the table.

"I like the ceramic tree on the bar top," he said.

Her first thought had been to have it on the table, but opted for the bar so it could be plugged in. She'd folded and wrinkled up more old Christmas cards to form a sort of holiday field around the tree. Bits of sparkle on the cards and from the confetti bits Kiernan urged her to save sprinkled atop them reflected the tree's lights.

Again, she smiled without looking at him. "Thanks." She tipped her head, considering the table. "I'll be right back."

She headed for the store.

He followed.

He'd blown it before by not going with her into the store. Wasn't going to do that again.

First, opportunities for the two of them to be alone without an entourage were few and far between. Second, she'd been different when she came back from her earlier trip to the store. More distant. All that smiling and not looking.

He wasn't letting that distance get even worse.

As he passed the store's cooler, something caught his eye.

CHAPTER THIRTY-FIVE

On her second go-round of the store, Bexley left the jerky aisle with a sigh, turned the corner into the candy aisle, and ran into Kiernan's back.

She rebounded away, nearly losing her balance. Then nearly losing it a second time for an entirely different reason when he grasped her arm.

"Kiernan. What are you doing here?"

"Looking for you."

"I'm still searching. Haven't found what I want yet. Something to put around the bottom of the trees and candles, so they're not just on a plain plate. But all I see so far is jerky." That all sounded like nervous babbling to her. Probably sounded worse to him. "The table—?"

"Can wait a bit. I want to talk to you. To tell you… I've watched you, Bexley. I've watched you make Christmas—"

"We all have. The food, the decorations, the—"

Shaking his head from her first word of protest, he added words now. "None of it would have happened without you. Without your ideas, your vision, your determination to give the kids a Christmas. To give us all a Christmas."

He stopped shaking his head, his words coming faster.

"And I don't know exactly how, but it's opened my eyes. I've realized how things went wrong, how I let them go wrong—not only with Felicity, but with other relationships, too.

"I do want what Cahill and Eleanor have, what the Curricks and their friends have. I suppose what my mother and father had or she wouldn't have mourned so hard for him. But I didn't go about it right.

"I don't think it's what you said last night about my being afraid.

Not entirely, anyway. Though watching Mom made me cautious, for certain. To be sure the good would be worth the sorrow if the worst happened."

She touched his hand. An instinctive gesture of compassion for him, for his family.

Before she could retract her hand, he turned his over, enclosing hers, palm to palm. Then he covered their joined hands with his other, not holding her, but, above and below her, warming her throughout.

"But even more than caution, I thought what Cahill and Eleanor and the others have would come to me pre-made. Like Christmas always has before—arrive in a complete package with little to no effort from me. Come, sit here with me so we can truly talk."

He used his hold on her hand to draw her down to sit beside him, backs against the shelves.

"Ah," she said wisely. "Because you were used to women throwing themselves at you and doing all the work, while you were like a Roman emperor, giving thumbs up or—"

He protested, "I wouldn't say that—"

"—thumbs down. Until along came Felicity."

"That's not exactly—" His frown shifted to a rueful smile. "I suppose so."

"But didn't she play hard to get?"

"Ah, that was part of my pre-made package. A woman who didn't ask too much of me, because sometimes she backed off faster than me."

"Because she was using you, stringing you along to get to Jack?"

"She was. So she never backed off too far, never backed off out of reach. Unlike you."

She tried to slide her hand from behind his. He held on. "Me? Are you blaming me for—"

"Not blaming a'tall. Explaining that when you did back away, a man expecting a pre-made relationship didn't know the next step of making one, as I wouldn't have known how to make a Christmas here."

"I suppose I did run off," she acknowledged slowly. "Though it wasn't because I expected everything to fall in my lap."

"No, it was because you thought you were done with relationships and I'd just given you another reason for that resolution."

"And you *had.*" Tart words, but she didn't try to withdraw her hand.

"I know. I'm sorry."

"I am, too. Too bad we couldn't have talked then like we are now."

"Wouldn't've done a bit of good." Her head snapped back at his cheerful pessimism. "We were neither of us ready for it."

"So, we should be grateful for being snowbound and missing Christmas with our families because we're past the awkwardness after last summer's, uh... after last summer and now we can be friends?"

"Friends."

She was not reading anything into that tone. Far, far too dangerous.

In a low, certain voice, he said, "I am over her, you know."

And she wasn't reading anything into his segueing from their being friends to his saying he was over Felicity. Talk about dangerous. No, she'd not read anything into tone or transitions.

"I believe you," she said slowly. "But sometimes the effects linger after the person—"

"What about your snooty ex, the eejit? Aren't you—?"

"I was. We've both let those crappy people haunt us. Why? Crazy. Letting them butt into our lives still when they were otherwise firmly in our pasts." She slanted him a quick look, then away. "Past time we shake off any vestiges of them influencing our lives."

"Good plan." He twisted away from her, reaching into his far pocket, and in the process resting their hand sandwich on her thigh, the weight and warmth sparking a deeper warmth.

He twisted back, facing her now, holding something over her head.

She tipped back to get a look at it. Green. At least greenish. "What *is* that?"

"Mistletoe."

"Mistletoe? I don't think—It's *not* mistletoe. Is that lettuce?"

"Mistletoe," he said firmly.

Then he kissed her.

Firmly and oh-so-wonderfully.

His mouth—the feel of him, the taste of him—was like coming home.

She wanted to give herself up to the sensation, to the moment … to him.

But she'd done that once before.

She pulled back.

"Wha—Why did you do that?"

"Shaking off the last vestiges. And because I've been wanting to for five months and more."

He kissed her again. Not even pretending she could resist, she kissed him back.

He released her hand. She used the freedom to touch his hair, his neck, on the way to winding her arm around him. And he certainly had other things to do with his hands.

"Bexley! Kiernan! Where are you?"

She pulled back with a gasp at Molly's call.

"Just a minute." She stood. "I'll be right there, Molly."

"Wait." Kiernan grabbed her hand. "A solution to your quest."

She looked down at him. His grin didn't entirely hide a frustration that caused a *ker-thump* in her chest.

He drew out a package of M&Ms from a nearby shelf. "If you use the red and green ones…"

"Yes. That's great." Back in practical mode—what had he called it? *Making Christmas?*—she added, "But make it Skittles. That way it's not Molly's initial or anyone else's. Get all the packages."

CHAPTER THIRTY-SIX

Kiernan held the bulk of the small candy packages, with Bexley carrying the overflow. "We have another little project and the meatloaf—"

"Is in the oven," Pauline said. "Now, put down whatever that is and sit down. You and Kiernan. Molly and Lizzie have something to say to you all."

Kiernan unloaded the packets atop the bar.

They took the two open chairs in a semicircle centered on the wood stove.

"Since you're too old for Santa, we wanted to give you some things, too," Lizzie said. "Things you missed from being here."

Molly stepped forward and put a paper towel-wrapped lump in Kiernan's hands.

He drew in a long breath appreciatively, calling attention to the fragrant warmth emanating from the lump.

"It's Irish soda bread," she said.

"I can smell that. It's marvelous. Thank you, girls." One side of his mouth lifted. "And Pauline."

"They did all the work."

"She told us what to do," Lizzie said. "There weren't as many ingredients as the cookies. No chocolate chips at all."

Pauline, suddenly the object of looks from all the adults, said, "Yes, I used my phone to find a recipe. Had to stand on the ladder in that back room, but I did it. And it's already fully recharged, so I didn't risk a thing."

Molly, ignoring that side issue, took a box with a perky bow to Eric.

He grinned at the sight of the box, but did a good job of delighted surprise when he got the ribbon off and announced, "My favorite cookies."

"They're store bought," Lizzie confessed. "Not like the chocolate chip cookies."

"Those are my second-favorite cookies," he assured her solemnly.

"Pauline made a batch while we were making the bread, so there are more of those, too. And she gave us these to give to you so you'd have your favorite ones," Molly said. "See? It says that place you mentioned."

"Andersonville. But how…?" he asked Pauline.

"Had them shipped out and planned to give them to you before I left for Chicago, but with the storm and you insisting on driving me…"

Eric thanked the girls, then kissed Pauline on the cheek with a hard hug.

Molly regained her role as master of ceremonies. "It's past Christmas Eve, but we're going to sing a song for Bexley."

Their two voices rose in a sweet rendition of *The First Noel.*

Even the storm seemed to appreciate it, hushing completely.

At the end, Bexley applauded enthusiastically and hugged them each. "That was wonderful, girls."

Lizzie said, "Next time, you all can sing with us. Like Bexley's family does."

Molly brought them back the point. "Next is Pauline. We can't go to church at midnight, because that's past, too—"

"And we can't go anywhere anyhow," Lizzie inserted.

"—so we said a prayer for your husband who died, along with Mommy, last night. We think they might be spending Christmas together."

Pauline swallowed, then smiled. "That's a very good thought. I believe they are."

"We didn't know about Gramps. See, we didn't get anything for Bobby or Dan or Daddy, but they're family, so maybe that's okay? Since Gramps is our grandfather and that makes him family, we thought that would be okay. But we didn't really know him before this, so then that's not like family. So we made more soda bread for him—us and Pauline—because his grandmother was Irish, like Kiernan."

She gestured for her sister to get on the other side of Gramps' chair, then Lizzie handed him the loaf.

"Well. Ah. That's—"

Molly ruthlessly cut through his attempts to speak. "And for the family part, we're adding this."

The girls threw their arms around him from each side, kissing him on his cheeks, which burned bright red.

Bobby, seeing the lovefest, used Gramps' red sweater as a hand-hold and climbed up into his lap, kissing him on the nose.

"I'm not doing that," Dan declared, his voice's register jumping high.

"Da—darned right you're not."

But Gramps looked up at his grandson and winked. The boy grinned back.

Never had meatloaf been so festive.

Dan didn't betray the presence of spinach and ate enough to please any cook.

Kiernan insisted his Irish soda bread be part of the meal, too, and Gramps followed suit. With the salad made from deconstructed sandwiches, butter-drowned boxed potatoes, black and green olives rounding out the meal, everyone was sated.

Until the cookies came out and they found room for more.

The second batch of chocolate chips, supplemented by Eric's special Swedish cookies, created a feast.

Gramps even voluntarily brought out his brandy for small toasts by the grownups.

They stoked the fire and sat around the table, passing the cookies, eating the Skittles not used in the decorations, and singing Christmas songs.

When Kiernan joined Lizzie and Molly on *Rudolph the Red-Nosed*

Reindeer, Bexley's mouth fell open. He had a wonderful voice. Warm and emotional and true.

With a glint in her eyes, Pauline suggested *O Holy Night* next. She, Bexley, and Eric started with Kiernan, but quickly dropped out, leaving him to complete it solo.

They all sat silent a beat as the last note faded.

"Wow." Molly's single word conveyed everyone's reaction.

"Why didn't you tell us you could sing like that?" Pauline's voice skidded toward scolding, but she wiped at her eyes, so no one was fooled.

"My brother Cahill's the musician in the family. He sang at Val and Jack's wedding, you know."

He looked at Bexley, somehow making those simple words string a connection between them that, again, *ker-thumped* her heart.

Ah, yes, because it had to do with far more than words.

Aware of Pauline looking from Kiernan to her, Bexley dropped her gaze, grateful he filled in the silence.

"I provide harmony now and then. Now, if we had Cahill here, especially with his guitar, he'd not let us waste all this time before the next song."

"What do you want to sing next, Kiernan?" Lizzie asked.

"God Rest Ye Merry Gentlemen."

He led them on an up-tempo version of that carol that segued into song after song. Occasionally lyrics received a new twist because no one remembered the precise words, but the spirit came through.

CHAPTER THIRTY-SEVEN

December 26

Even the littles slept in the next morning.

As Bexley enjoyed the luxury of waking without a mental list of to-dos and how-tos scrolling through her brain, she abruptly recognized the quiet from outside. Perhaps the abated wind contributed to all sleeping so well.

As they roused, one by one, they were as slow-going as bears coming out of hibernation, though distinctly more cheerful.

Heading for the bar room for a coffee cup they'd missed washing last night, Bexley encountered Kiernan in the back aisle of the store.

There was nothing cold about his eyes now.

In fact, they were hot enough to make her feel oddly shy. "Morning."

"Good morning." He looked behind him, then circled her arm and drew her down the side aisle and back to where they'd been yesterday, amid the candy. "Bexley. You're wrong."

With her mind still occupied by Christmas, she looked around, but the depleted supplies of candy didn't tell her much. "What? Did we miss something—?"

"Yes." He turned her toward him, cupping her face in his palms. "Or nearly. We've nearly missed each other."

"But—"

"C'mere." He drew her down to sit beside him on the floor, tight against his side, his arms around her. "What you're wrong about is me. I'm over Felicity. I want you to be sure of it. Not a doubt. I was in July, too. Or the first sight of you wouldn't have… But I was too busy tripping over my own feet to see straight. When we were together, *that* was the truth."

Kiernan kissed her ear, then moved his head farther back, until she felt his mouth at the back of her neck, his warmth caught between the raised collar of her top and her nape. He kissed and kissed and kissed. She shivered with the sensation, all along her skin. He opened his mouth over the spot and she felt the scrape of his teeth in a gentle stroke of a bite. Then he sucked the spot. And the shivers dove deep into her core, shuddering there in pleasure.

They kissed. Slow. Exploring. Combustible.

She felt the tangible proof of his desire against her as he drew her onto his lap.

Footsteps jolted them apart, Bexley abruptly sitting next to Kiernan, instead of mostly on him.

Lizzie peered around the corner of the shelves at them. "*There* you are."

If they had to be interrupted, Bexley was grateful their interrupter wasn't one of the adults or Dan, none of whom would have missed the atmosphere or their positions.

"Pauline says you need to come in the bar room now."

Kiernan groaned low. "Two for two—matched set of tormenters."

"Okay, Lizzie, I'm coming right now. Kiernan's, uh, going to stay here a second." She bit the inside of her cheeks to stop a giggle.

"Yes, I am," he muttered.

"But he has to help set the table and Pauline says you're cooking the breakfast because you're the only one who knows how the pieces go together. He *has* to come."

"He will," Bexley said. "You have to be patient."

"I *am* patient." Lizzie's affront echoed in her voice. "Molly's the one who's not patient."

"It's a good thing you're the one who came for Kiernan, then, isn't it?"

Bexley started to stand.

Kiernan held onto her arm, keeping her half-bent toward him. He looked up into her face. "When we're alone."

She returned the promise. "Yes. When we're alone."

Pauline organized breakfast preparations, with Bexley's job to cook the main dish in the skillet. "And nothing more. The rest of us will handle everything else. Many hands make light work."

As Bexley and Pauline left the bar room, heading toward the kitchen, the older woman said, "What is that sound?"

"It sounds like… It is. It's a plow. Passing by on the highway. I can see the top of it."

"Plow?" Pauline turned her head back to the bar room, announcing. "There's a plow."

"P'ow! P'ow!" Bobby enthused.

The others piled to the store windows and door, Dan holding up Bobby so he could see between the signs. Kiernan and Bexley hung back, exchanging a look.

Was he also wondering if what happened between them here could survive outside this cocoon?

They heard the plow several more times as they ate the spicy breakfast Bexley created from shredded sandwich beef, salsa, eggs, bread crumbles, and more spices. She'd made extra, hoping it would hold everyone until dinner, because the lunch makings were sparse.

Returning to the bar room after cleaning up, Bexley heard a closer scraping sound. She almost didn't tell the others. But it wouldn't have delayed the inevitable by much.

Again, they all went to the store.

"Shoveling us out," Gramps said.

The same trooper from three days ago, finished a narrow path to the store's door.

Gramps opened the door. "Stamp your boots, don't track that snow in here."

"Same old Gramps. You'll never—" The trooper's mouth stayed open a second. "Well, I'll be. You cleaned up nice, Gramps."

"He looks like Santa, doesn't he?" Molly asked, slipping one hand into her grandfather's.

The trooper looked from that hand to Gramps to the rest of them ranged behind him, then back to Molly. "He does."

"Would you like breakfast?" Pauline asked.

"Breakfast?" His gaze flickered toward the shelves.

"A real breakfast," she amended. "Our Bexley is an imaginative cook, among other talents. Molly, will you run and get the breakfast? Lizzie, get the trooper a place-setting and, Dan, will you pour him a cup of hot coffee, please."

In short order, the trooper was seated at the table, with reheated Tex-Mex scramble on his plate and a steaming cup of coffee at hand. Instead of eating, though, he stared around the bar room.

"Haven't seen this place look this good since…" He glanced toward Gramps, then veered away, clearly knowing better than to step into Winnie territory. "Haven't ever seen it this festive. How'd your propane hold out?"

"Have plenty."

"Plenty? What?" Pauline demanded of Gramps. "You insisted we bring in that firewood for heat and spread out showers and not do laundry to make sure we didn't run out of propane."

"Not so *we* didn't run out. So *I* won't run out before the next delivery. Rather use up that firewood. Shame we couldn't have used up what was in the shed, too. But I'll put that back out front when we have a melt and it'll sell."

"You—You—"

"What? You got no cause to complain. You like having us all together. Seems to me you all had a fine time."

Before Pauline could recover, Molly said, "We did."

"We had Christmas," Lizzie confided to the trooper.

"I see that. Looks like a real nice Christmas, too."

"Santa came," Molly added. "He found us here. Not Gramps, even though he looks like him now, but the real Santa."

"Let the trooper eat, girls," Pauline instructed. "And then we can ask our questions."

After he cleaned the plate, he told them the eastbound Interstate was open, while westbound should be passable in a few hours. The short stretch of highway to the entrance ramp was passable. And the plow was coming back to open the way to the gas pump so locals could access it as they dug out.

That meant when they could clear their cars, they could be on their way.

"Oh." Molly and Lizzie sighed out harmonized disappointment in the syllable. "You're all leaving."

Kiernan, standing behind them, put an affectionate hand on each girl's shoulder.

"You won't be here all that much longer either, girls." The trooper took in both girls, Dan, and Gramps with his look. "Hall Quick contacted our office. He kept trying to get through to you, Gramps, but your landline's down. If you'd get a cell phone like everyone else… Anyway, he made it to Dakota—the fool—sold his cattle by pushing ahead of the storm, then got stuck when he tried to turn back. Though it doesn't sound like he had as nice a time of it as you folks. Where he's at is still closed, but he should be able to head back tomorrow and pick you all up to go home."

"Don't worry, Gramps," Lizzie said. "We'll come back."

The old man blinked hard. "I don't need—"

"Of course you do," Pauline interrupted. "And I'll be back to make sure you're keeping this place as it should be."

Pauline and Eric opted not to resume their trip to Chicago, planning to return to their homes in Bardville as the roads west cleared.

Bexley and Kiernan gathered their things to leave, Bexley sharing a few meal ideas with Pauline as she packed.

It seemed like it should have taken longer, considering all that had happened.

Exchanges of addresses, emails, social media IDs, and phone numbers accompanied promises to stay in touch.

Then exchanges of hugs with Bobby, the girls, Pauline, and Eric. Handshakes with Dan and Gramps.

Kiernan and Eric came back in from loading the vehicle.

"It was…" Bexley's throat closed. She tried again. "It was a very merry Christmas. Thank you. Each and every one of you."

In the vehicle, their seat belts on, the engine warming the interior, Kiernan paused before putting it in gear, his gaze on the steering wheel.

"Bexley, I want you to know… It wasn't being stranded. It wasn't Christmas. It wasn't even watching how you *made* Christmas. It's you. It's all of you."

He turned to face her.

"I want to make Christmas and every other day with you, Bexley Farber, and I hope you feel the same. I believe you do."

"I… I do."

"Will you take me home to meet your family? Will you come to Gloucester to meet mine?"

She leaned toward him, their lips so close.

"Yes."

Then she kissed him.

It was a several minutes before they left the snowy lot. As they passed the shop's door, they saw all the others standing there—obvious witnesses to the kisses—grinning and waving.

EPILOGUE

Kiernan and Bexley reached her family's home December 27, after a mid-trip overnight stop at the third place they tried, the others filled by travelers staying put for now.

Kiernan looked around the routine motel room. "We could wait for someplace more romantic, before—"

She grabbed a fistful of his shirt from under his chin and tried to draw him to her. Since he didn't budge, it had the effect of drawing her up to him. That worked, too.

"Are you *nuts?*" she growled into his face.

After a startled beat, he grinned. "I am. Indeed I am." He kissed her fast, then scooped her up.

They spent three delightful and tormenting days—separate beds—at her family home. He fit in right off. When they caught him cheating at Scrabble, he was declared to be one of them.

But on the thirtieth, they started east again for her turn to meet the clan.

"Easier for you than it was for me," he said when she wobbled a bit with nerves as she drove across Northern Indiana, "you've a glowing report already from Val and Matty."

She turned startled eyes to him. Then jerked them back to the road. "What do you mean?"

"Last summer. News of that was through them all like—" He swallowed a colorful phrase. "Right away."

She groaned.

"I'm not saying this visit wouldn't have been difficult for you after walking out on me—"

"After I—?"

"—but they'll forgive you now they see I've done the same."

"*You've* forgiven *me*—"

"I have."

Eyes still on the traffic, she reached out her right arm and whacked him in the upper arm. Between her angle and his coat, it lacked punch.

"If rough's your fancy, Bexley, I must be telling you it's not mine. But best to sort out such matters when we're in the hotel I've booked for tonight, not while that walloping great semi is trying to sit in our backseat."

She focused on the important issue while expertly evading the semi with no sense of personal space. "The hotel you've booked?"

But he would say no more of it.

Their bedroom at the historic inn near Syracuse had a working fireplace, the flames visible from the bed, which proved convenient because that's where they spent most of their stay. They took time for a delicious dinner, but had breakfast in bed.

That breakfast tray came with a single white rose.

As they prepared to leave, Kiernan detached six white petals and starburst them around a pat of butter.

"What are you doing?" she asked.

"Have you ever heard of pasque flowers?"

"I don't think so."

"They can bloom in the snow."

"That's nice."

He drew her down to him. "Very nice."

The stay at the inn fortified them for the final hours driving in light snow to reach Gloucester, Massachusetts, and another inn—this one owned and run by Kiernan's sister-in-law and brother.

They arrived mid-afternoon, also finding Val and Jack and their children there, as well as Val's exuberant relatives.

By midnight, it was clear to all that the New Year would be entirely happy.

Sitting in front of a bright fire, the three women who'd cooked New

Year's dinner relaxed while the men cleaned up with the dubious help of the next generation.

"I think our first experiment turned out fine," Val said.

Bexley surveyed the satisfied smile of Val Trimarco Ralston. Her cousin, Eleanor, frowned at Val.

"What experiment?" Bexley asked.

"Rebecca calls it the Wyoming Marriage Association, though we've agreed marriage isn't necessary to declare a situation finalized."

"Rebecca… She's from Far Hills Ranch?" She remembered Dan Quick saying their ranch wasn't far from Far Hills.

"Right. She's married to Luke, the foreman. And there's Ellyn and Griff, Kendra and Daniel. And Marti and Robert, who own the home ranch, though they don't live there. That's why they've used it for special occasions for people in the area, a few weddings, a couple reunions."

"That's the Wyoming Marriage Association?"

"No, no. Rebecca hopes to find matches for guys who keep showing up because they were used to camping out with Luke when he was single. Good guys, but they need help to, you know, make a real romantic connection."

"Val and several others believe they can provide that help." Eleanor's tone combined skepticism and affection.

"We can. We did. We—"

"Val."

At her cousin's warning word, she stopped abruptly.

Looking into the flames, Bexley asked, "Kiernan and me? We were the experiment?"

"It's not like we *planned* for you two to be snowbound—that was pure good luck."

Eleanor coughed.

"Well, it was. Gave them more time to figure things out than the car trip alone would have. Though when Matty texted the drive was a possibility, I told her she had to make it happen."

"Val, hush while you're ahead. Let Bexley absorb this."

Bexley was silent for a full minute.

She blinked three times, coming back to the room. "I have two candidates."

"Women?"

"Men. Because I'm pretty sure Pauline's taken care of herself with Gramps."

"I don't know," Val said. "Rebecca won't want to make matches for new guys until she cuts down the bachelors hanging around her house."

"As your first experiment, I deserve to pick next. Besides, wait until you hear about these two."

And there, on the shore of the Atlantic Ocean, began discussions that led Eric Larkin and Hall Quick—and his children—into completely new lives as the next projects of the Wyoming Marriage Association.

Thank you for reading Kiernan and Bexley's story!

**Get ready for the upcoming
Wyoming Marriage Association series.**

Bexley and other women of the Wyoming Wildflowers series team up with those from the Bardville, Wyoming, and A Place Called Home trilogies in the Wyoming Marriage Association series. Be sure to catch up on those series before you read what's in store for Eric Larkin and Hall Quick.

Bardville, Wyoming

Unexpected love arrives when strangers come to small-town Bardville.

A Stranger in the Family

A Stranger to Love

The Rancher Meets His Match

A Place Called Home

Three cousins share a family ranch … and a century-old family curse that only they can lift.

Lost and Found Groom

At the Heart's Command

Hidden in a Heartbeat

Kiernan, Bexley, and friends ask if you'll help spread the word about them and the Wyoming Wildflowers series. You have the power to do that in two quick ways:

Recommend the book and the series to your friends and/or the whole wide world on social media. Shouting from rooftops is particularly appreciated.

Review the book. Take a few minutes to write an honest review and it can make a huge difference. As you likely know, it's the single best way for your fellow readers to find books they'll enjoy, too.

To me—as an author and a reader—the goal is always to find a good author-reader match. By sharing your reading experience through recommendations and reviews, you become a vital matchmaker. ☺

For news about upcoming books, as well as other titles and news, join Patricia McLinn's Readers List and receive her twice-monthly free newsletter.

www.patriciamclinn.com/readers-list

The Wyoming Wildflowers series

Donna and Ed's lives are worlds apart. Can they ever bridge the distance…

Wyoming Wildflowers: The Beginning

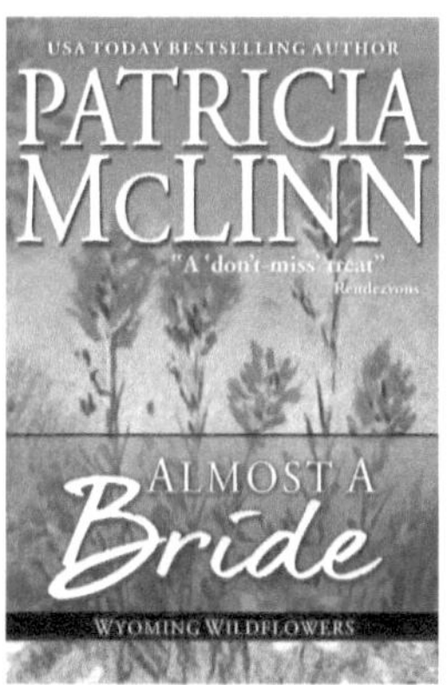

Dave Currick has everything he wants, except the woman he loves…

Almost a Bride

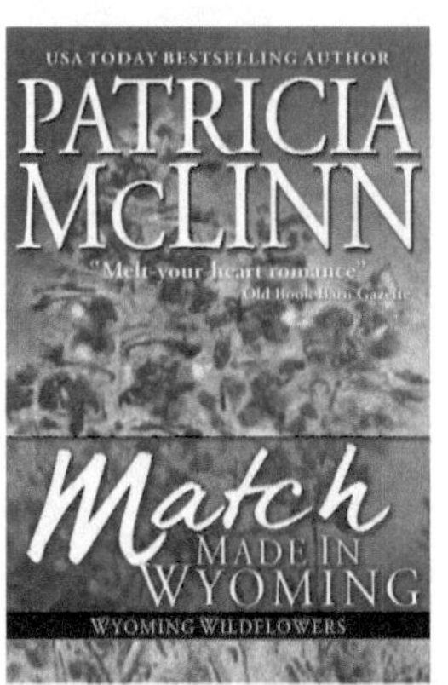

Cal and Taylor can spark a wildfire, but will they come together in…

Match Made in Wyoming

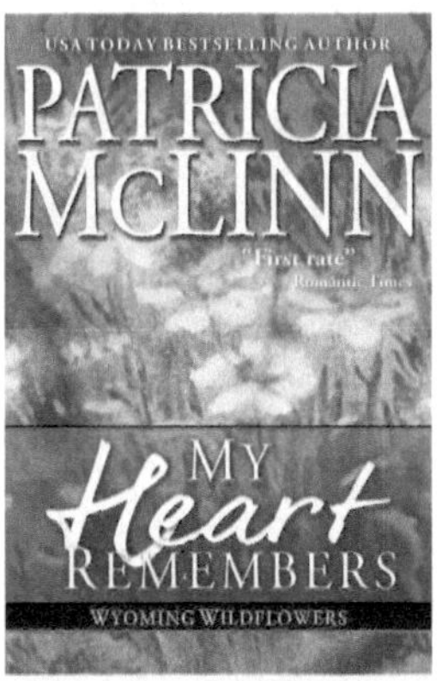

Lisa's carried a secret in her heart for years—and he just hit town…

My Heart Remembers

Prequel to Jack's Heart

A New World

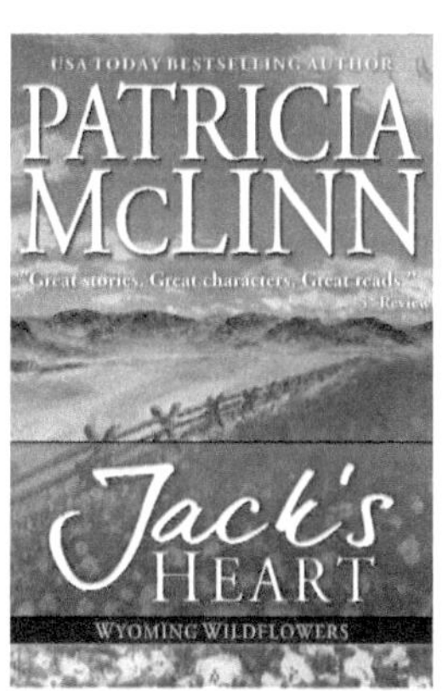

New England single mom meets her Lone Ranger.

Jack's Heart

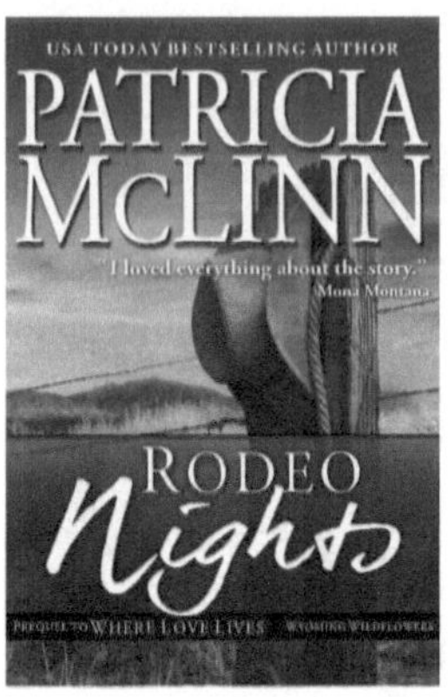

Prequel to Where Love Lives
Rodeo Nights

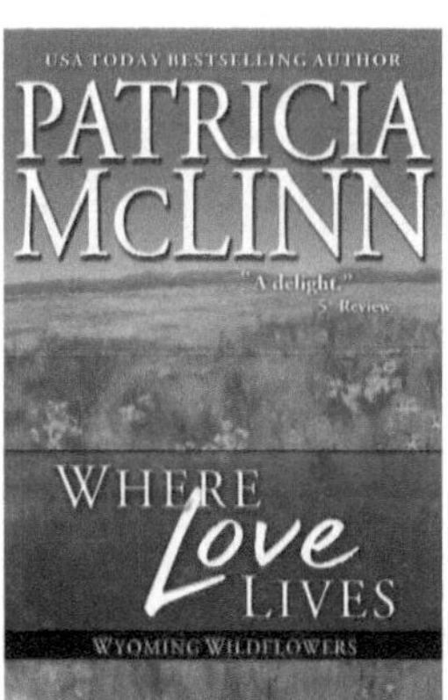

One night stands in the way of Zoe and Matt spending the rest of their days together.
Where Love Lives

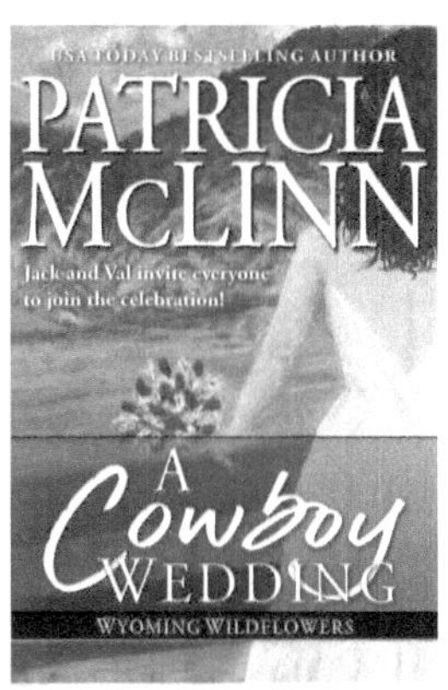

Jack and Val invite you to share the big day with them.

A Cowboy Wedding

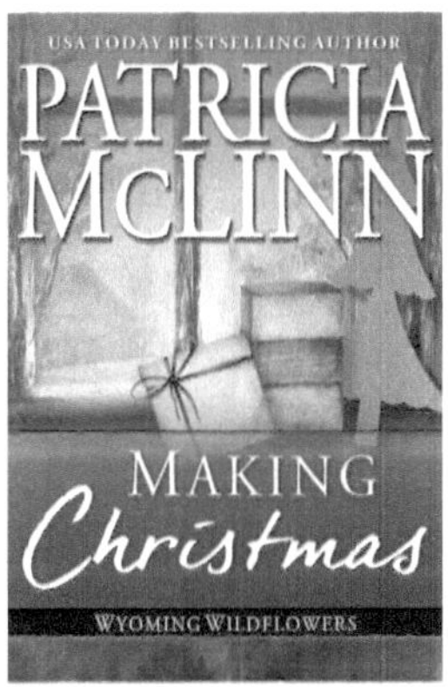

Ho ho uh-oh! Can they rescue an accidental noel?

Making Christmas

Box Sets (ebook only)

Wyoming Wildflowers Trilogy (Books 2-4)

Wyoming Wildflowers Box Set Two: A New World (prequel) and Jack's Heart

Wyoming Wildflowers Box Set Three: Rodeo Nights (prequel) and Where Love Lives

Wyoming Wildflowers: The Complete Collection

Eight books: The Beginning, five central titles and two prequels. Perfect for new fans who have dipped their toes into a field of wildflowers and now want to binge-read these stand-alone stories.

Also by Patricia McLinn

Seasons in a Small Town

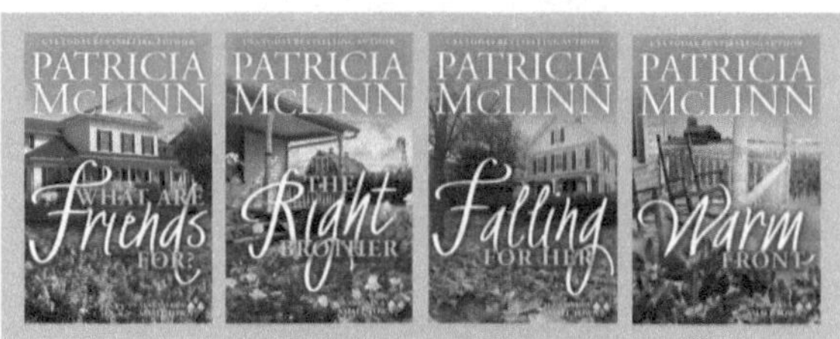

What Are Friends For? (Spring)

The Right Brother (Summer)

Falling for Her (Autumn)

Warm Front (Winter)

Marry Me series

Wedding of the Century

The Unexpected Wedding Guest

A Most Unlikely Wedding

Baby Blues and Wedding Bells

The Wedding Series

Prelude to a Wedding

Wedding Party

Grady's Wedding

The Runaway Bride

The Christmas Princess

Hoops (prequel to The Surprise Princess)

The Surprise Princess

Not a Family Man (prequel to The Forgotten Prince)

The Forgotten Prince

About the Author

USA Today bestselling author Patricia McLinn spent more than 20 years as an editor at The Washington Post after stints as a sports writer (Rockford, Ill.) and assistant sports editor (Charlotte, N.C.). She received BA and MSJ degrees from Northwestern University.

McLinn is the author of more than 50 published novels, which are cited by readers and reviewers for wit and vivid characterization. Her books include mysteries, romantic suspense, contemporary romance, historical romance and women's fiction. They have topped bestseller lists and won numerous awards.

She has spoken about writing from Melbourne, Australia, to Washington, D.C., including being a guest speaker at the Smithsonian Institution.

Now living in northern Kentucky, McLinn loves to hear from readers through her website and social media.

Visit with Patricia:

Website: patriciamclinn.com

Facebook: facebook.com/PatriciaMcLinn

Twitter: @PatriciaMcLinn

Pinterest: pinterest.com/patriciamclinn

Instagram: instagram.com/patriciamclinnauthor

www.ingramcontent.com/pod-product-compliance
Lightning Source LLC
Chambersburg PA
CBHW020815190726

48285CB00006B/2295